Our Last Fall

Ulwich Preparatory Academy: One

S Bolanos

CHAOTIC NEUTRAL PRESS LLC

Contents

Content Warnings

Ulwich Preparatory Academy is a mature new adult prep school series and contains situations that some readers might find offensive. It is intended for audiences 18+ and features violence, sex, and blatant homophobia. This series also deals with themes of identity, self-doubt, consent, safe sex, and abuse*.

*There will never be on-page depictions of sexual assault

Chapter 1

Four Years Ago

Andy

The room filled with a mild glow as I pulled back the curtains. It was still beyond gloomy, but the moonlight would have to suffice; turning on so much as a lamp would be too risky. My hands closed around the cardboard box. It immediately began jerking as I picked it up off the floor and placed it on the desk.

Out of habit, I looked towards the other bed in the room. It was just as empty as it had been yesterday. *Talk about a stroke of luck.* Of course, I doubted Lucien felt lucky since he was the one with chicken pox. We hadn't even had time to get properly acquainted after being moved into the upper level student wing together before he'd had to leave.

I placed a large textbook on top of the box to make sure the lid didn't pop open and send the box's contents spewing across the room. Now that the container was secure, I picked up the piece of paper that had been hidden beneath it. Even in the almost nonexistent light, I could make out scratch marks crisscrossing the page.

Trying to write a letter was stupid.

I crumpled the scarred page, then shoved it deep in the wastebasket beneath countless other similar scraps.

He deserves to hear it from me, anyway.

I glanced at the clock. He'd be here soon. I needlessly adjusted the box, which hopped in response.

Deep breath. He's your best friend. He'll understand. Okay, maybe he won't understand exactly, but he'll still appreciate the honesty. Yeah, the honesty. I can do this.

I shook my hands in a vain attempt to dispel my nervous energy.

"What are you doing?"

I jumped in place and spun around at the whisper. "Mitch. You scared the crap out of me," I whispered back.

He shrugged as he carefully closed the door. "Did you get them?" he asked as he crossed the room to set his own supplies on the bed. The large container of chalk dust shone in the light. "This is going to be our best prank yet. Were you able to get the frogs?" he repeated.

I stood there like a statue, my mini pep-talk already a distant memory.

I can't do this.

"Hello. Earth to Andy. Did you get them or not?"

Mitch is staring at me. I should tell him they're in the box under our Social Studies text.

He lifted his eyebrows and held out his hands, impatience clear on his face.

"I'm gay." My eyes widened in horror. *Fuck.*

"Okay, but did you get the frogs?" Mitch insisted.

"Did you hear what I said?"

"Yeah. Now, are you gonna answer the question?"

"But—don't you have anything to say?" I asked, confused.

The light of the moon flashed against the whites of his eyes as he rolled them. "Does you being gay change who you are? Does it make you a different person than the one who helped me plan this?"

"Well, no."

"Then were you able to get the frogs or not? Because this is going to be a super shitty prank without them."

"They're in the box on the desk," I replied, still in a mild state of shock.

His trademark mischief quickly replaced his exasperated expression. He tossed me the container full of white dust and walked over to admire our prize.

"I got twelve," I added to make up for my earlier lack of response.

"Perfect." He removed the book and carefully picked up the box, which gave a characteristic jolt. "We better get going or we'll miss our window."

Present Day

Andy

I stared up at the vaulted ceiling of the cafeteria. The deep red brick and exposed beams lent the large space a grandeur far exceeding the room's use, but I'd stopped being impressed years ago. Despite Ulwich Preparatory Academy's mission of excellence and only accepting young men from the most prestigious families, it was still a school like any other.

"You gonna be studying with Connor again this year?"

I shifted my focus to my friend as he put his tray away and dusted his hands of the nonexistent crumbs. Calvin Bridges was meticulous to a fault and not one to make a mess—ever. Even his dark curly hair, while cut into a long shag that definitely violated school policy, was precisely styled to give the impression of nonchalance. His navy school blazer hung over a perfectly pressed cream button down and intentionally crooked tie striped with the Academy's colors.

As literally one of a dozen students of color in the entire school, his choices undoubtedly made a statement, loud and clear and one no one dared to call him on. Despite his rebellious appearance, or perhaps because of it, he was also the school's unofficial keeper of secrets.

I emptied the remains of my breakfast into the trash before responding. "Let him take care of his own homework for a while."

Calvin snickered. "Bet he didn't like that."

"Don't say it like that. It was as much his idea as it was mine." Connor and I had had a good thing going for a while, but as one year turned to two, our easy relationship had become strained.

"Sure it was, Andy," he responded with an over-the-top eye roll. We turned to exit the cafeteria together to steal a few minutes outdoors before the second bell and the day's classes.

I glanced back towards a group of guys sitting on a table by the windows. The light illuminated the rowdy crowd as they laughed and carried on. The one at the heart ran his hand through light brown hair and smiled. Mitchum Hudson: Ulwich Academy's star lacrosse player. Athletic perfection and so far out of reach, he might as well have been on another planet.

Pain stabbed through my chest like it did anytime I saw him.

Why did I have to tell him? If I had just kept my stupid mouth shut. If I hadn't…

Calvin gripped my shoulder, dragging me back to the reality that I was standing in the doorway and blatantly staring across the cafeteria.

"I'm coming," I grumbled.

"It's been four years," Calvin whispered.

"I know. And not a single word in between." I pushed open the door to the courtyard with a tad too much force. It rebounded off the outside wall, then nearly crashed into a too-slow Calvin.

"You guys were already drifting apart. You said so yourself."

I cast Calvin a sour look.

"Don't get mad at me for telling it like it is," he said as we settled into our usual spot on the green beside a low stone wall that I was sure served a purpose at some point. "He's a typical jock, just like the rest of them. All muscle, no brain."

I raised an eyebrow. "Unlike us?"

"Unlike you. I'll be lucky if I can pass Algebra II with a low C. You're the brainiac." He stood up on the low wall and struck a classic Shakespearean pose. "I'm doomed to be a starving artist. Forever suffering for my creations, sacrificing my very soul, with no hope of recognition." He paused and glanced down at me to make sure I was paying attention. "Or more importantly, compensation."

The dramatic declaration had the desired effect—I laughed. "Get down from there before you break something."

He snorted. "I think the wall can take it."

I laughed again. "Not the wall, more like your neck."

He waved away my concern, then mimicked walking a tightrope complete with balancing arm swings. I shook my head. Calvin may not have been the same kind of friend Mitch had been, but he was still a good one. Not to mention he understood things Mitch never would.

The Mitch you knew is gone, I reminded myself.

"Look what the cat coughed up." The taunting comment snatched me out of my musings.

I raised my head from the notebook I was scanning to find the school bully headed our way. "It's too early for this shit," I mumbled. Meanwhile, Calvin was already turning to confront him. I sighed inwardly.

Just once couldn't they leave well enough alone?

"If it isn't Benjamin Price himself, come to wish us good morning. Look Andy, he brought the welcome wagon and everything," Calvin said with far too much cheer.

Benny's face immediately twisted at the abundance of enthusiasm; Calvin wasn't *supposed* to be excited to see him. "They should ship your queer ass back to where it came from," Benny sneered.

"Are you offering to pay the postage? You could even wrap me up yourself," Calvin responded with a wicked smile.

Benny's expression clouded with anger. "As if I would go anywhere near a cocksucker like you."

Calvin feigned a wound to the chest, then bold as brass declared, "If I'm not mistaken, most of the guys here would do just about anything to have their cocks sucked. Present company not excluded."

Benny's cheek twitched and his lackeys looked at each other askance. Calvin had hit a little too close to the truth for their comfort. Going to an all-boys boarding school did leave certain things wanting. Finally, Benny recovered and fired back, "You think you're special, because your senator mom got you into this school, but we all know the truth—she's nothing more than a mail-order-bride that used daddy's money to make a name for herself."

Calvin vaulted off the low wall to land practically on top of Benny. "My mother got what she was owed and even an idiot like you should know you have to be a citizen to be a senator."

"Who'd she have to fuck to get those papers? No wonder you're such a queer."

"*My mom*?" Calvin's voice pitched high with incredulity. "What kind of shit did your dad make *your* mommy agree to in that prenup? Tell me, was she pregnant before or after signing away her life?"

"Fuck you, you fucking fudge-packer," Benny snarled.

Point Calvin.

"You kiss your mother with that mouth?" Calvin crossed his arms and popped a hip. "Or have you even seen her since daddy got his heir?"

"One of these days, I'm going to put you in your place, you fucking hapa faggot."

"Just be sure to shower first," Calvin said, cool as a stone.

I checked my reaction and watched Benny struggle to contain his. Behind him, Neil and Todd looked confused at their leader's sudden lack of comeback.

"Motherfucking fairy," Benny mumbled before signaling to his companions.

"Which is it Benny? Am I a motherfucker or a faggot?" Calvin called after them. Benny kept walking, not deigning to respond. Calvin continued to hold his ground until the trio was out of sight.

"You shouldn't goad him. One of these days, he really will do something," I cautioned as I adjusted the notebook on my knee.

Calvin scoffed before joining me on the ground. "Benjamin Price hates himself more than he hates me."

Mitch

I watched the door to the mess hall close behind Anderson Gallagher, obscuring his bright copper hair.

He's friends with Calvin now. He won't ever be mine, not after what I did.

Boisterous laughter erupted around me, directly contradicting my depressing thoughts. I withdrew deeper into myself to escape the offensive sound that had taken complete possession of my life over the last four years. At first it hadn't been so bad. These people were my friends. They cared about me and wanted me to succeed. But as time went by and their expectations chipped at my soul, I realized how horribly wrong I'd been to believe they were friends, because they weren't, not really, not the way Andy had been.

I miss the way things used to be.

A sharp smack landed on my arm and jolted me out of the downward spiral. I returned my attention to the table full of familiar faces, not a one of which knew a damn thing about the real me. "What?" I asked, having lost all track of whatever ridiculous conversation we were having this morning.

"Trixie, man," Brian repeated. An image of a girl with bottled-red hair came to mind. It hung about her sun-deprived face in a pixie cut that wasn't doing her any favors.

My brow furrowed. I hadn't talked to or even thought about her since school dismissed for summer. "What about her?"

"Bro, are you even listening?" Kyle asked, his peach face a mask of exasperation.

"You two still hooking up or what?" Brian repeated. He crossed brown arms made that much darker from a summer spent outdoors over his chest and leaned back with a raised eyebrow. I scanned the eager expressions surrounding me and my stomach turned. Dating Trixie had been an awful decision that I never would have made in the first place if it hadn't been for these relentless assholes.

I shrugged as if she was the furthest thing from my mind, not the least of which because she was. "No, not really," I replied honestly, Beatrix Roberts held zero interest for me and always had. Her stick figure topped with disproportionately large breasts made her look like a cartoon with the personality to match. She'd started with blonde hair that had miraculously turned an awful shade of red when I'd made the mistake of saying I preferred redheads in one of many attempts to break up with her.

"See, I told you," Nate said with all the righteousness of someone proving a point that doesn't need proving.

"Whatever." Aaron rolled blue eyes that had snagged their fair share of the student body at the Mary Barnes School for Distinguished Young Women. "Still doesn't mean you can try."

"Why not?" Nate asked. I couldn't help but be surprised that he of all people had an interest in pursuing Trixie. As my roommate, he'd gotten more exposure to her than the rest and should know she wasn't worth the drama. Then I remembered Nate was a self-professed "boob-guy".

John snagged the toast from my forgotten tray. "It's the bro-code."

I stared down at where the rest of my morning meal remained untouched. If I didn't start eating more, I wouldn't make weight and wouldn't be allowed to start come season in the spring. I pushed at the disconcerting yellow mass of eggs with my fork, but couldn't bring myself to take a bite.

"Not to mention, you don't stand a chance," Brian added, uncrossing his arms and leaning forward to smirk at Nate.

Would it be so bad if I couldn't play anymore?

I looked around at my teammates. They were loud, crude, completely obsessed with the neighboring girl's school, and totally oblivious.

This school is doing a terrible job of turning us into gentlemen.

Nate turned to me and dragged me away from my thoughts yet again. "So, what do you say, Mitch?"

"About what?" I responded, looking once again at the several faces all eagerly awaiting a response and reminded myself for the millionth time to try harder not to sit in the middle.

"Do you think Nate has a right to go after Trixie if you two aren't dating anymore?" John asked.

I shrugged again. "I don't care what you do. Go after her if you want," I replied, genuinely not caring. Nate pumped his fist in the air, much to John's annoyance. "But I'll warn you, she has zero sense of humor."

Nate made a rude noise. "I'm not interested in her sense of humor." The table erupted into guffaws and I glanced back at the door where Andy had disappeared.

Chapter 2

Four Years Ago

Andy

Everything had gone perfectly. More than perfectly. When Mr. Hanover opened his desk drawer tomorrow morning the whole school would hear about it.

"The room is going to be a total disaster," I said, closing the door softly behind me.

"Hanover is going to freak. It'll take weeks to get chalk off of everything," Mitch added emphatically, his eyes sparkling in the glow still coming from the open window. He plopped down on my bed and I walked over to join him. I was too wound up to sit though, so I remained standing.

"You were right," I said. "This is definitely our best prank yet."

"I still can't believe no one has figured out it's us."

"Why would they? We're awesome," I stated, then quickly had to suppress a bout of laughter. It really was unbelievable that no one had guessed it was us after two whole years. I may have been doing pranks at Ulwich since before Mitch transferred in, but they were small time compared to the mischief we got up to together.

Tonight is going so well. The prank went perfect. I told Mitch the truth—most of it anyway. And we're still cool.

"It was a brilliant plan," I said, taking another step closer.

Mitch shook his head, laughing quietly to himself. "I may have come up with the frogs, but you're the reason we never get caught," Mitch countered.

"Pft, I almost got caught plenty of times before you got here."

"Yeah, but you didn't."

"Fair point." I smiled at Mitch who smiled in return. I loved it when he did that, it brightened his whole face and made my insides flutter.

Mitch leaned forward, his eyes shining with merriment. "Can you just see Hanover's face?"

"It's gonna be epic," I said, mirroring his lean in my enthusiasm. One beat passed, then another, as we stared at each other so close we were sharing the same air, grinning from ear to ear. My heart flipped as something between us seemed to thicken.

I blinked and suddenly our lips were pressed together. I hadn't planned for it to happen, it just had. Time seemed to slow as my brain processed the fact that I was actually kissing him, something that I'd barely been brave enough to dream about, and...and it was *perfect*.

Mitch pulled away and time rushed to catch up. "What the fuck," he hissed. His gaze fell on everything but me.

What have I done?

"I've known you're gay for all of two hours." The angry words hit me like a slap in the face.

"I...I...Mitch, I'm sorry. I didn't mean..." I stepped further back with each word.

What have I done?

Mitch's hand shot out lightning fast to stop me. His grip on my wrist tightened to the point of pain and panic seized my heart at the wild look shining from my best friend's eyes. Likely former best friend now.

I swallowed hard. "Mitch, please. I'm sorry. I won't tell anyone. I won't do it again. It was stupid. Please, you have to believe me. I swear." I pulled in vain against his hold as his eyes bored into me. Mitch had always been bigger than me and thanks to lacrosse tryouts, he was now definitely stronger.

He still hadn't said a word. Just that intense gaze that felt like it was skinning me where I stood.

Tears welled in my eyes at the betrayal I'd committed. "Mitch, I'm sorry. Maybe I didn't tell you everything like I should have. But I *swear* I won't breathe a word," I pleaded.

Present Day

Mitch

"Are you coming?" Brian asked as he walked backwards out of the school into the sunlight. John, Nate, and Kyle all glanced over their shoulders in anticipation of my response. I hiked my bag higher up my shoulder and willed myself to keep walking. But I didn't. I remained rooted inside the threshold shrouded in shadow, just out of reach of the afternoon sun.

Nate stopped walking and turned to face me fully, his features twisted into a frown. "Something up?"

Doubt flooded through me at the concern in his voice. Maybe I wasn't doing such a good job of hiding my depression from my roommate as I thought. To my horror, the others pulled to a stop as well, apparently incapable of going anywhere without me in tow, least of all to the informal practice that Coach S had all but ordered our first day back.

"What gives man?" John asked, the painfully bright light shining off his overly greased, dark hair.

I swallowed hard and scrambled for words that wouldn't come. My gaze darted between the four of them all staring at me, waiting for an answer. My grip tightened around the strap of my bag while my heart hammered in my chest. The harder I tried to speak, the more strained my breathing became until I stood there panting quick breaths that only made my pulse spike more. Just the thought of stepping onto the practice field again, of listening to the coach yell and shout and demand, made me want to throw up all of the nothing I'd eaten for breakfast and lunch. Not even the hope of getting benched brought a reprieve, because I *wouldn't* get benched. Coach would force me to eat, just like he'd made Carter lose fourteen pounds in a week in order to make the semifinals last year.

Brian's eyes narrowed and he took a step back toward the school. "What's the deal?"

Panic surged through me and finally brought my voice. "I'll be there in a bit, I just remembered I have to stop by Nolan's office."

I took a step back and hoped none of them would dig deeper into the lie.

"Nolan's a prick. Just don't take too long or Coach'll freak." Brian waved for the others to keep moving and I bit back a sigh of relief.

"Yeah," I said, then quickly turned and retreated into the school before one of them decided to join me.

My bag slipped as I rounded a corner so fast my shoes squeaked on the hardwood floors. I fumbled to keep it from flying and ended up with my back pressed against the wall, clutching the bag to my chest and gulping for air. A few precious seconds ticked by and my breaths came a little easier, but they stopped altogether when the sound of approaching footsteps filled the hallway.

I slung the bag over my body this time and took off down the hall once more. I needed to go somewhere I could cool down, somewhere no one would find me. My destination swam into view and I took the steps two at a time, ascending the Tower as fast as my feet would carry me. At last I stood in the center of the circular room facing the massive opening that hadn't held glass for as long as I'd been here. I gasped out a sob that the draft immediately stole and dropped the nearly empty sack to the ground with trembling hands. Tears stung my eyes as I gazed out the would-be window at the green beyond. Already the tiny dots of my teammates scurried about in coordinated patterns.

"I can't do it anymore. I can't live like this." The tears I'd been fighting for what felt like four fucking years finally slipped free as I stepped toward the ledge. The dizzying thirty-foot drop to the ground below swam before my eyes.

Another sob tore free as I stumbled back away from the ledge. I fisted my hands in my hair, desperate for an escape, but too afraid to take the one right in front of me. I sank to the floor in a defeated heap and buried my head in my arms.

Andy

I finished shoving the assortment of textbooks and paperbacks into my bag, then slung the worn strap over my shoulder. The first day back was always grueling. Between getting books organized, establishing a schedule with my college mentor, having to hear about everyone's summer excursions... seeing Mitch... I needed some space.

"I thought you said you weren't studying with Connor anymore," Calvin called out when I was almost to the stairs.

I turned back to face him. "And I'm not. I'm allowed to want to be on my own, you know."

"That's not why you're going up there." The flat statement just missed being a rebuke. Rather than dignify the accusation with a response, I turned back to the stairs.

My foot hovered over the first step as I glanced up the passage. *The Tower*. That's what everyone called it, mostly due to the steps that curved up and to the right until they disappeared; not to mention the huge window at the top. Despite the allure of the name and stunning view, hardly anyone ventured up there. No one wanted to climb all of the damn stairs, which made it the perfect place to go if you wanted to be alone. That was how it had become Mitch and my hangout all those years ago. It was the birthplace of some of our wildest schemes.

I wet my lips.

Will going up there make seeing him this morning hurt any less? I should go with Calvin to the library, or the courtyard, or literally anywhere else.

Despite the logic, I lowered my foot and began the climb. Fifty steps later, I rounded the final corner and started. To my surprise, another student was already there. My shoulders slumped.

So much for being alone.

It was hard to tell who it might be with their back to me. Their focus was centered on the vast window and it didn't seem like they'd noticed my arrival. It looked like they might have been there a while already as they were seated on the floor with their legs stretched out, their school blazer tossed casually beside them. Curious, I took a step closer. It wasn't until my bag hit the floor and he raised his head that I realized I recognized him.

"Mitch? What are you doing here?"

His arm lifted and moved as if wiping something from his face.

Is he crying?

"I could ask you the same thing," he said over his shoulder.

"I come up here sometimes. To think. You know?"

"Yeah," he replied softly without answering my initial question and returned to gazing back out the opening.

I should go.

My fingers wrapped around the canvas strap of my messenger bag fully prepared to do just that. I looked from it to Mitch.

I definitely should go.

Still I hesitated.

But something is clearly wrong.

The strap slid through my fingers back to the ground and I walked towards him. After another moment of indecision, I sat down. We hadn't spoken in years, but that didn't eliminate the reflex to comfort my best friend, even if I didn't have a right to call him that anymore. "Is everything alright?"

He shrugged and continued to stare out at the green landscape below.

To the north, I could just make out the lacrosse fields filled with scurrying bodies. From this distance, they looked like ants. "Aren't you supposed to be at practice?"

"Yeah," he said evenly, still not looking at me.

"Won't you get in trouble for missing it?"

"Probably."

I pulled my knees up and rested my arms on them, not sure how to proceed.

I really should leave. He's not my Mitch anymore. It's not like I know anything about his problems.

I glanced at him out of the corner of my eye.

Then again, he hasn't left yet either.

I took a deep breath and let it out slowly. "Do you wanna talk about it?"

He turned to look at me. His hazel eyes were rimmed with red, reaffirming my belief that he'd been crying. He stared at me for a long minute before turning away.

Way to fucking go, Andy. What am I thinking? We haven't even been in the same vicinity for this long in four years. Not since that night.

Heat burned across my face at the memory.

"I can't stand it." His sudden speech startled me right out of my creeping blush. "There's no pleasing any of them. They all want more from me, but none of them actually want *me*—not the real me. I'm not sure I even remember who that is anymore," he added in a whisper.

"I didn't realize you were so unhappy." He'd certainly never looked that way, always laughing, surrounded by his brainless friends.

"No one does. No one cares."

My hands fidgeted in my lap. "I care," I said quietly.

Why did I say that?

"Sometimes I wish I'd never gone out for the team."

I thought back to all those years ago when he'd first told me he was going to try out. He'd been so excited to be doing something his father had done when *he'd* attended Ulwich. I'd been happy for him, even as I recognized it was signaling the end. "You always wanted to be on the team," I responded.

Mitch shook his head. "I didn't know what it would mean. The things I would lose." That last was so soft, I barely even heard him.

"What do you mean?"

He looked at me and I had to grip my fingers to keep them from fidgeting again as he searched my face.

I let out the breath I was holding when he finally shifted his intense focus to the window.

"It never ends. All I do is practice, play, and work out. I'm barely even passing my classes. I can't afford to fail, but when am I supposed to study with the whole damn team constantly on my back? Not that it would matter if I *did* fail," he added bitterly. "The grades would just get doctored. Can't lose our lead attackman, can we?" He stood abruptly.

Unsure of what to do, I remained seated.

"Mitch, you need to push harder. Mitch, you need to lead the team. Mitch, you have to win," he said as he paced the small room. "And that's just the coach. My fucking teammates are worse." He gestured emphatically as he continued to rant. "Their humor is gross and they're obsessed with getting laid. Not that any of them ever do, but it doesn't stop them from expecting me to sleep with every girl within twenty miles."

I glanced towards the stairwell. His voice had been getting louder with each grievance. Just because no one came up here didn't mean someone at the bottom couldn't hear the echoed conversation. "Mitch…"

"I can't take it. I just wanna go back to the way things used to be, when I was allowed to be a person. Not just some piece of meat to be ground down until there's nothing left. Fucking assholes don't give a shit about anyone but themselves."

"Mitch…" I tried again already moving to retrieve my abandoned satchel.

He's going to get himself in trouble if he keeps on like this. Even if someone from the team doesn't hear, word 'll get back.

"I mean, fuck them. Their idea of a good time is going on a panty-raid at the neighboring girl's school or fucking tea-bagging each other. It's disgusting. Do you remember how much fun we used to have? We didn't do any of that stupid shit. We—"

"Mitch.".

He spun on me. "What?"

I slung the strap across my body.

His eyes darted between the bursting satchel back to me. "Where are you going?"

"Somewhere else."

His face fell like he couldn't believe I'd have the audacity to walk out on him.

I rolled my eyes and gestured to the stairs. "Are you coming?"

At this hour, hardly anyone was in the corridors and we passed through them relatively unobserved. I walked at a good clip, turning down first one hallway, then another and another, until at last I reached my destination. A quick glance showed the passageway was empty.

I walked right up to an over-sized portrait of Walter Ulwich, the founder of the academy, and pulled it away from the wall. Mitch strode purposefully through the opening and I followed behind, letting the giant painting swing shut behind me.

Mitch flicked an equally hidden switch, and the room filled with a soft, yellow glow. "I think I'm going to quit the team."

I set my bag down and let out a sigh. "Why would you do that?"

"Because I hate it. I hate *them*."

"You don't hate them. I know they can be jerks, but they depend on you."

"I don't see why that has to be my responsibility," he said angrily, glaring at the floor.

I stepped deeper into the secret room and placed a hand on his slumped shoulders. "That aside, you're really good. You can't deny that."

"I don't even like lacrosse. How can I be good at something I don't even like?"

"Natural skill?" I offered.

"I miss the way things used to be." His gaze lifted to meet mine. Although his eyes were still red, there was a hardness to them. "Before I—" He shook his head.

I gave his shoulder a reassuring squeeze. "You've been play-ing for a long time."

"Pretending," he corrected. "I've been pretending for a long time. I never had to pretend with you." His gaze softened as he looked back at me.

I searched his sad eyes, at a loss for how to make this better. We hadn't been close in years, since the last time we'd been in this exact room, but I hated to see him hurting like this. My thumb stroked the tiny patch of exposed skin it rested on. He was warm—probably from working himself up—and he felt good. He'd felt good then, too.

I didn't realize the distance between us had been shrinking until Mitch's mouth was on mine. My hand reflexively left his shoulder to curl around the back of his neck while his arm slid around my waist and pulled me closer even as he kissed harder. I sighed into it and he took advantage of the opening to slip his tongue past my lips.

The shock of it finally gave my brain a chance to catch up. I pulled away and put both of my hands between us. The distance, however, was minimal as his hand stayed firmly planted on my waist. "W-What are you doing?" I stuttered.

His face clouded with confusion. "What do you mean? *You* brought *me* here, Andy."

I pushed against his chest, and he finally let go. "Yeah, so you could vent without anyone overhearing." I took a small step back, still struggling to pull it together.

He licked his lips, and I tried not to think about why they were so pink. "But…"

I can't do this, not again. I don't even know why I brought him here.

"I was just trying to make you feel better," I reiterated, not sure which of us I was trying to convince.

His eyes searched my obviously panicked face.

I nervously wet my lips. They still tasted like him.

He took a full step towards me, forcing my arm to bend and effectively invading my personal space.

I stiffened.

His eyes bored into me, and mine widened in fear.

"What if this *is* what I need to feel better?" He said the words softly, but there was an edge to them, a hardness I was afraid to entertain. Mitch was my best friend—four years couldn't change that—but he was also trouble.

Can I play this game with him?

When I failed to respond, he moved my hand out of the way and captured my mouth again. For reasons that eluded me, I kissed back. The almost soft kiss became more exploratory. My eyelids fluttered as my heart beat erratically. Kissing Mitch felt even better than I remembered. He'd gotten better at it. We both had.

What am I doing? This is a mistake. I know better. This can only end one way.

The knowledge didn't change the fact that I'd wanted this for years, still wanted it.

I can't lose him again because of my selfishness. I have to tell him no.

I pulled away again, but he was less than inclined to relinquish his hold on me a second time. His hazel eyes were super intense as I stared into them.

Say no, Andy. Tell. Him. No.

"Fine." The traitorous word was out of my mouth before I could call it back.

His eyes lidded and he leaned forward.

I quickly sandwiched a hand between us, and he stopped short. "But no sex." At least one lesson I could remember, even if I was barely holding onto it with a white-knuckled grip.

"Okay," Mitch said, leaning forward.

"I mean it, Mitch. Absolutely no sex."

If it doesn't go that far, if I don't repeat the same mistake, then it can't end the same way.

He searched my face for a moment, and my anxiety ratcheted up several notches. It was already too late. That was what he wanted from me. A quick escape, a way to ease his troubles for an afternoon before returning to his reality. I just got him back and now I was losing him all over again for the same damn reason.

"No sex," he finally responded, then promptly recaptured my mouth. There was nothing tentative about the kiss. It was harsh and needy, and I gave it to him. His arm tightened around me once more. I wriggled my hand free and wrapped it around his head, urging him deeper.

This is a very bad idea.

His grip on my waist shifted, and he pushed me against the wall. I let out a gasp at the sharp contact. Before I could say anything, his mouth closed back over mine and his body pressed firmly against me. There was no hiding my groan *or* my growing erection. His teeth pulled at my bottom lip as he freed my top two buttons in quick succession.

"Mitch." Despite how breathless I was, the warning tone was evident.

"I fucking heard you, Andy. No sex." His fingers slipped beneath my collar to caress the now exposed part of my neck.

Feeling his touch on the sensitive skin made me want to feel it everywhere. I desperately tried to rein in my rampant hormones before I did something I would regret even more.

He abandoned my mouth, and I gave a soft moan as his wet lips replaced his hand.

Oh fuck.

His fingers dug into my hips and I realized I wasn't the only one struggling. His lips found mine again, and I was lost, so totally freaking lost.

Oh God Mitch.

Despite my adamant assertion not to let this go too far, I was already a heartbeat away from letting him have whatever he wanted. If he wanted head, he could have it. If he wanted to bend me over something, he could fucking do that too. My fear of consequences was systematically being seared away with each heated second. I clung to him, desperately wanting to hang on to something I'd thought I'd lost forever.

Gradually the kiss faded from outright demanding to light presses until at last he gave them up altogether and rested his forehead against mine. His heavy breathing mirrored my own and, for once in my life, I had literally no words. I could barely even hear myself think over my pounding heart.

"You should go first," he whispered. He was still so close, the air itself felt like a kiss.

"What?" I asked, still trapped in a fog.

He leaned away and looked me in the eye. "You should leave first."

"Oh. Right." I cleared my throat and stepped aside, since he was crowding me. He silently watched me redo the buttons he'd popped, his gaze staying on me as I stooped to retrieve my bag. I did a quick inventory of myself to make sure I was back in order before walking to the secret entrance. I opened the door just enough to peer into the outside hallway. When I was sure the way was clear, I opened it further.

"I'll see you around, Andy."

My heart skipped at Mitch's words. I wanted to look back, but didn't trust myself to actually leave if I did.

What the fuck have I gotten myself into?

Chapter 3

Four Years Ago

Andy

"Come with me." Mitch's words sounded like a death knell in the quiet room.

He's going to kill me.

Icy terror washed through me at the realization. Then Mitch tugged me toward the door and I immediately began clawing at his hand.

"Please. I'm sorry. It won't ever happen again. I swear." My desperate pleas fell on deaf ears. I dug my feet into the area rug. It wrinkled, but didn't offer any resistance. Mitch continued to pull, relentlessly dragging us to the only escape. I tripped over the bump I'd made in the rug and stumbled out the door. I glanced back at my room receding behind us and renewed my frantic attempts to get free.

"Mitch. Stop. I promise I won't say anything. No one will ever know. It'll just be between us. Please," I cried.

Mitch lurched to a stop and used his grip on my arm to pull me closer. "Do you wanna get caught?" he hissed.

I quickly ran through the possibilities. If I made enough noise and attracted a teacher or prefect, then I might be spared. However, then they would want to know what we were doing out of bed after lights out. That could potentially be way worse, especially if they checked the classrooms. I swallowed and quickly shook my head.

"Good. Now be quiet or we'll both be on the chopping block." I barely registered his concern for getting caught before he tugged on my arm again. Once more, I was being towed by Mitch to what was surely my end.

Present Day

Mitch

I hadn't meant to kiss Andy, I really *really* hadn't, but clearly, I was just as incapable of making good decisions now as I had been four years ago. My tongue darted out to taste my lips. I could still feel him there, buzzing beneath the surface. When he'd shown up in the tower, I hadn't known what to make of it. When was the last time we'd exchanged more than a passing glance, let alone spoke? Then he'd… stayed. That had thrown me even more.

My finger tipped the corner of the photograph taken a lifetime ago as I sat on my bed with my legs stretched out—mercifully alone. Within its faded edges, two thirteen-year-old boys laughed with a joy that only ever seemed to come with summer. It was also the first summer I hadn't felt so horribly alone since my dad died. When he'd died in combat two years before, I thought I'd never be happy again. Then came Andy. I'd been at Ulwich all of a year and we'd been inseparable since the moment we'd met on my first day. We'd had the time of our lives getting into all sorts of trouble with never a thought that our fast friendship might come to a sudden terrible end. My smile at the memory slipped, and I chewed on my bottom lip as I continued to stare at the frozen memory.

Andy's eyes sparkled with joy as he leaned across the frame to shove me. Their bright green had been darker in the secret room. Whatever he said, I recognized lust when I saw it. I shifted on my bed, increasingly uncomfortable in my school khakis as I remembered how he'd reacted. The press of his full lips against mine. The molding of his hard yet remarkably soft body. The whisper of a moan as I'd sucked on his neck.

A groan spilled out as I recalled how fucking aroused he'd been, his hard length digging into my thigh while a flush stained his pale skin and darkened his freckles. I palmed my straining dick and focused on his eyes, only they weren't the bright green shining back at me, but ones darkened with want.

His dragging me into the secret room should have been a second chance, an opportunity to get it right this time, but of course I'd fucked it up…again. All I had to do was *not* kiss him. It shouldn't have been that hard. Who was I fucking kidding? Andy pressed buttons on me no prior hookup had ever found. And fuck me if I hadn't done my damnedest to find someone who could. But no one could replace Andy with his snark and being too smart for his own good. That fiery hair that defiantly proclaimed his Irish roots. And those eyes. *Fuck*, those eyes.

I couldn't take it anymore. The hand not holding the picture fumbled with my pants. I needed a release like I needed air to breathe. My fingers wrapped around my pulsing shaft and my head fell back with a groan that came straight from my balls. Absently, I considered digging out some lotion or *something* to make the slide smoother, but I didn't have the patience for it. I stroked once and squeezed the base, nearly choking on another groan. My head popped back up, and I zeroed back in on those insane eyes, memories driving my hand faster. The slight burn of the dry friction only made me more desperate. My breaths came in short pants as fantasy overlaid the memory.

Back in the secret room, Andy wasn't clothed this time, but gloriously naked, all of his smooth skin on display and free for the touching. He curled his fingers in my hair as he pressed his ass back against me. I sucked bruises into his delicate skin until he turned to look at me over his shoulder, eyes darkened with lust, lips parted in invitation. The ache in my balls turned painful as I dug fingers into his sides and yanked him back to claim that mouth.

Pain turned to tingles as I kept fueling the fire, still unable to look away from the photo clutched in my hand. My toes curled in anticipation of the release I so badly needed. It burned beneath my skin, threatening to turn me to ash if I didn't do something soon. I stroked faster and faster, each pass of my fist bringing me closer. A few more seconds, that's all I needed. Just a few more seconds, then I could finally explode.

My balls tightened, and I braced myself for what promised to be an epic finish. Then the door opened. In a blind panic, I shoved the picture out of sight and fell on my side, struggling to put myself away as fast as humanly possible, the oversight of lube now a blessing.

"Jesus fucking Christ, Nate! Knock much?" I finished zipping my pants and glanced up to find my roommate not even remotely apologetic about having walked in on me rubbing one out.

"Don't you fucking start with me," he snapped right back, the slight pink in his round cheeks the only sign that he might be embarrassed. "You don't want to be disturbed? Put a fucking sock on the door like a normal person." He slammed said door shut and stalked over to his own bed and desk. His book satchel landed in the chair with an angry squeak that matched his bad attitude perfectly.

"Excuse the fuck out of me. Last I knew, you were supposed to be somewhere else." My heart pounded as I bickered with him about dorm etiquette. Had he seen what I'd been holding? Had I ruined the picture when I shoved it under the comforter? Nate couldn't know, no one could fucking know. I grabbed at my hair and continued to silently freak out while Nate bitched about his shit day. If he'd seen, if he even suspected, forget not wanting to play anymore, the entire team would fucking crucify me. And if they found out I'd been getting off on a picture of Andy...they'd kill him.

"Hey, you okay?"

The sudden expression of concern ripped me out of my spiral. "What?"

"I asked, are you okay? Look, I get that it's embarrassing as shit to get caught, but it's not that big a deal. Really." He shrugged as he tossed his school blazer over the chair. "Could be worse. Ever been caught by your grandma? Now that shit is fucked up." He laughed, and I knew I was supposed to too, but I couldn't.

"I'm gonna go for a walk. Cool off." I slid off the bed and toed my shoes back on.

Nate's face fell, and he pushed his brown hair back. "Yeah. Okay."

I didn't give him any more information, just walked out of the room without a backward glance. For once, the usually bustling hall was empty. I briefly contemplated going back up to the Tower, but dismissed it when I remembered why I'd gone the last time. With a huff, I turned down an adjoining corridor, walking fast enough to look like I had a purpose, except I had no idea where I was going. My thoughts strayed to the picture that lay hidden beneath my sheets, possibly ruined, for anyone to find. Why had I taken it out? I was always so careful with the damn thing. I doubt even Andy knew I had it, since my mom was the one who'd taken the picture.

After long enough that my legs were actually getting tired, I slowed and sagged against a wall. I wasn't even surprised to find myself facing the East dormitories where Andy's own room was. My fingers dragged across my face and I let out a heavy breath. I'd spent four years trying to let him go and was obviously failing miserably. I glanced down the deserted hall, now shrouded in shadow. Lights out had come and gone while I'd wandered aimlessly through the school in search of an answer I already knew.

"What the fuck do you think you're doing, Hudson?"

Great, just what I needed right now. "Cool your tits, Price."

"What the fuck did you say to me?" Benny asked, bowing up. With his broad shoulders, he made an excellent Midfielder and could probably beat me to a pulp if he wanted to get his hands dirty. Oh, I'd put up a good fight and get my licks in too, but Benny would win hands down.

I sighed and straightened up. Being a hot mess didn't give me license to be stupid. "I said, I'm going to bed."

Benny stepped aside so I could do just that. "You think you're untouchable because you're coach's shiny star."

I couldn't help but glance over at him. Benny fought hard for his position on the team. Benny fought hard for everything. But he'd never have the talent I did. "Aren't I?"

A muscle in his cheek twitched as I passed, but he didn't stop me or say anything else. My own words played in my mind as I made my way to bed. *Aren't I?*

I slipped into the room and let out a relieved breath when the sound of Nate's snoring filled my ears. I shut the door softly behind me with barely even a click, then tiptoed over to the side of my bed and flicked on the lamp. A quick glance showed the light hadn't disturbed him. Reassured, I fished out the photo. Crinkles marred the delicate paper, and I carefully smoothed them out. All in all, it could have been worse. At least I could still see Andy's face clearly. Plus, if I was lucky, my mom had made duplicates and I could get another.

I stole another glance at Nate, then made my way to the closet. Propped at the back was my dad's old army duffel. Mostly by feel and memory, I replaced the damning photo in between the lining and put the bag back exactly how it was with hardly a speck of dust out of place.

In silence, I stripped down to my boxers and undershirt, then slipped between the covers, my mind still circling what I didn't want to admit. I'd tried to let Andy go once. I couldn't do it again.

Andy

I sat my lunch tray on the table and swung my leg over the bench. I eyed the selection before me skeptically. It wasn't a gourmet meal by any stretch of the imagination, but there was one thing it never failed to be—nutritious.

Just once couldn't we have pizza or something?

I stabbed the seared chicken and set about turning it into manageable pieces. My fork was halfway to my mouth when the sight of another tray and its adjoining student manifested in front of me. The useless utensil clattered down, sending wrinkled green beans flying.

"This seat taken?" Mitch asked as he sat without waiting for a response. I glanced over at his usual table to see if everyone had miraculously vanished. Per usual, it was overflowing with rowdy guys pushing each other and laughing. My gaze swiveled back to Mitch.

"What are you doing here?" I hissed.

"Eating lunch with my friend. Is that alright with you?"

"Um, yes?"

Why is he really here? Any minute, the whole fucking team is going to descend on us. He'll be fine, but what will they do to me?

I shuddered at the possibilities.

"You cold?"

"What? No." I retrieved my fork, which had somehow held on to its piece of meat.

"So where's Bridges?" he asked, starting to eat as well.

"Uh, he's getting a lecture or something from the art professor."

Mitch nodded and took another bite.

We're really having lunch together. This is happening right now.

"He's pretty good from what I've seen." I was about to tell him I agreed when he asked, "So are you two…?"

It took me half a second longer than it should have for me to realize what he was blatantly asking in the middle of the cafeteria. I snorted a laugh. "Um, no. Calvin's a friend, that's all."

A smile spread across Mitch's face as he continued to demolish his lunch.

"What about you and—oh, what's her name?—Trixie, that's it."

He groaned. "Heard about that, did you?"

I laughed at the theatrics.

"Nothing there," he answered.

"Oh? What happened?" I prodded. That sounded suspiciously like a story.

He leaned back and scooted vegetables around his plate. "First off, she's absolutely insane."

I laughed again.

"I'm serious. Stay away from all the girls at that damn school. The lot of them are certifiable," he added with a short laugh.

"I think I can manage that just fine."

"You know, I was thinking with it being a new year and all, it might be nice to apply myself a little more," he said, shifting in his seat, his lunch forgotten.

"What did you have in mind?" I asked, leaning forward despite myself.

"I could really use some help with my history paper."

I let out a sigh and started gathering my trash. "If you're fishing to get me to write it for you, then you should know I don't do that sort of thing." I stood up, fully prepared to make a hasty exit and diligently working to hide my disappointment. Why did it have to hurt so much?

Mitch bumped his tray as he got up. "What? No. That's not what I meant at all."

I seriously doubted his request for a study partner had anything to do with the other option. I gave a huff, and against my better judgment, turned back to him.

"Andy, I already wrote the damn thing. I was just hoping you could look at it. I'm sure it's absolute trash, and it's not like the professor really expects anything from me, but just once, it'd be nice to turn in something halfway decent."

"Oh." *Well, I'm an ass.* "Yeah, I could do that."

Mitch looked visibly relieved. He mirrored me and gathered his tray, though it still held most of his meal. "Awesome. Meet in the courtyard tomorrow after practice?" he suggested as he walked with me to the bin.

I mentally ran through any potential conflicts. "That should be fine. You know where the low wall is on the east side?"

His eyes twinkled with mischief as he smiled. "How could I for-get?"

It took me a second to realize what he was referring to. When I did, I chuckled. We'd once set off a firework there. It was supposed to be for a prank, but it didn't work as we expected and we'd nearly lost a few fingers. "You know, there's still a blast mark," I said.

"No way."

I nodded. "God, I still don't know how we didn't get caught."

"Probably has something to do with the fact that we booked it out of there like we were on fire."

I laughed again, remembering some of our closer calls.

"So, I'll see you tomorrow then?"

I looked into his hazel eyes, the eyes of my best friend, the same one who had come up with so many of our wild schemes, and the one who had thought it was a good idea to test the firework first. "Yeah, I'll see you tomorrow."

"Cool." He promptly dumped what remained of his lunch and hopped back to join his goon buddies.

I stood there a moment, just appreciating the brilliant grin he'd given me before he left.

Maybe my Mitch isn't as gone as I thought he was.

I shook my head and turned to exit, immediately running into Calvin. "Oh, hey. You're done sooner than expected," I said, continuing my path out of the cafeteria.

He fell in step and the doors swung shut behind us. "Eh, doesn't mean it was any more pleasant to bear. I'm more interested in how *your* lunch went. Do my eyes deceive me, or was that the esteemed Mitch Hudson I just saw you with?"

I rolled my eyes.

"What did *he* want?" Calvin didn't even try to hide his over-the-top inquiry.

"He asked to study together."

Calvin guffawed loud enough to earn us a reproachful look from some passing teachers.

I waved an apology and turned down the nearest hallway. "It's not like that."

He continued to snicker.

"I'm serious. Cut it out." I considered telling him about what had happened the other day, but decided that wasn't liable to help my current situation.

"I'm sorry, it's just too good. First Connor, now Mitch. Keep going like this, and you'll be able to collect the whole set."

"Well, if it does turn into a recurring theme, it'll have to be an incomplete one. I'm not going anywhere near Benny."

"Good. Because *that one* is mine." He gave me a devilish grin before sauntering down another passageway toward his next class.

Chapter 4

Four Years Ago

Mitch

I shoved Andy into the secret room and closed the door. He stayed quiet for all of three seconds before words started spilling out of him.

"It won't happen again. I don't know what I was thinking. Not a word, I swear. Please don't kill me."

"Kill you? I'm not going to kill you," I snapped at him, more than a little upset that he would ever think that. Rather than be comforted, he blanched.

"W-what are you going to do? Please, I can make this right. Just give me a chance."

I shook my head. "Stop talking. I need a minute." I grasped my head, but it didn't do shit to stop my mind from spinning. Everything had happened so fast. I needed to wrap my head around it and I couldn't do that in his room while he was very loudly freaking out.

Andy's gay. How did I miss that? We spend practically every waking second together. How could I not know?

"You don't have to do this. I'm sorry. Mitch, please," Andy blubbered.

I dropped my hands and looked at him. My gut gave a sickening twist at seeing his wide eyes and pale face.

He's terrified.

I walked over to him, and he flinched. I grasped his arms before he could try to retreat again. As it was, he looked like he was trying to figure out how to make a play for the entrance. We both knew there was no way he'd get to it before me.

"It was an accident," he insisted, water welling in his eyes. That much I knew was true. It had been a total accident, one that couldn't be taken back.

"Stop talking," I said again and shook him, causing a tear to slide free.

"You don't have to talk to me anymore. I understand. Just please, don't hurt me," he pleaded. There it was again, this insane belief that he could ever do or say *anything* that would make me want to hurt my best friend.

"I'm not going to hurt you," I growled.

He pulled against my grip, his eyes still wide with fear and apologies spewing from his mouth. "I promise. I won't do it again. No one will ever know. Please—"

"For the love of God. For once in your life, Andy, stop talking." His mouth opened as if to keep going anyway. I jerked him toward me and mashed my mouth against his. He immediately went stock still. I kissed him harder, forcing my tongue past his salty lips.

He gave a small squeak, but didn't fight me. I released his upper arms to cradle his head and pull his face closer. Kissing Andy wasn't at all like I'd expected. I knew his lips were full, but I'd never imagined they'd be so soft, so pliable. Even trembling, they fit against mine in a way I hadn't experienced before.

His hand left my arm and rose shakily into the air. I braced myself for him to push me away. Instead, his fingers wrapped in my hair and forced my mouth harder against his. Then his lips finally moved. In a single heartbeat, everything shifted. My hands fell to his waist to pull his body tight against mine. Andy let out a gasp and arched into it. The kiss got wilder, and I groaned.

"Mitch," he whispered against my mouth. Whatever doubts I had vanished.

I silenced the rest of his words with a harsh kiss even as I frantically worked to remove his night clothes. I needed to feel his skin against mine, and I needed it now. The stupid fabric bunched and got stuck. I gave a growl of frustration, unwilling to stop kissing him long enough to get the damn thing off of him properly.

A sudden pressure on my shoulders forced me to take a step back. I met Andy's heated gaze as he reached back and pulled off his tangled shirt. It fell by the wayside, quickly followed by his pants. My mouth went dry. I'd seen Andy naked before, but not like this. Not flush and definitely not aroused. I swallowed past the unexpected lump in my throat and brought my gaze back up.

Andy's chest rose and fell with breathing heavy, not unlike my own, but he didn't look away. He'd meant what he'd said. Andy wasn't fucking with me. He really was gay.

Present Day

Mitch

I rubbed a hand along the back of my neck as I made my way down the hall. The last-minute change to meet inside had been necessary because of a surprise rain shower. For probably the hundredth time, I patted the bag at my side to reassure myself it was still there. Like I could somehow misplace the damn thing while it was strapped across my body. But it wasn't the bag that I was worried about so much as the paper within. What if Andy took one look at it and decided I was a hopeless cause? What if I really wasn't any better than mediocre? What if sports was really all I was good at? And the scariest thought of all—what if no matter what I did, I'd never be able to undo the sins of the past?

That last one smarted, and I rubbed at the familiar ache in my chest, my constant companion these last four years anytime I made the mistake of thinking of the friendship I'd lost, the one I'd ruined.

Get a grip. He's reading your paper. Probably going to give a few grammar tips and send you on your way.

Reality aside, it didn't stop my heart from lurching into my throat the moment I opened the classroom door. The locale had been my suggestion, but it wasn't helping my anxiety like I thought it would. If anything, knowing I would be alone in a room with Andy was actually making it worse.

He glanced up at my arrival and I nearly called it quits right there. I still didn't know what had possessed me to kiss him after all this time, let alone try to inhale him like the last air on Earth resided in his lungs. All I knew was that I'd been thinking about him, about us and what we'd been, and then he'd been there. He'd sat down, talked to me, and for a shining moment, I'd gotten a glimpse of the past before I'd wrecked it. Then he'd taken me to the secret room, and it was like history was doomed to repeat itself. There I was, making all the same mistakes. But it had been different this time. He'd put his foot down—mostly—set rules. It had been a stark reminder that in the four years we'd been apart, Andy had grown up. He wasn't the wide-eyed youth anymore. He was top of our class, knew his own mind, and had boundaries. Hell, even according to the state he wasn't a kid anymore, not since August ninth.

"You planning on standing there 'til the next bell?"

I took a deep breath and a fateful step forward. "No."

He crossed his arms over his chest and leaned back at my grumbled response. The move put him directly in the path of a ray of sunlight streaming through the window. The tension in my chest loosened. Andy had changed, but his eyes were just as green, his hair just as red.

Maybe redder.

A smile tugged at my lips as his eyebrows climbed up his forehead. Finally, he asked, "What's so funny?"

"Nothing." I ducked my head to hide the renegade grin and took a seat next to him. "Let's get this over with." I fished in my bag and pulled out my travesty of a report. The sad part was that I really had tried, and it was still awful. "Go easy on me."

He snagged the papers from my hand, barely missing giving me a paper cut. My eyes went wide as I spied the red pen already uncapped in his hand. "When have you ever known me to go easy on anyone?"

"Look, I know it's probably the worst thing ever, but you could at least sugarcoat it for me."

"No can do. If you want sugar, Mr. Isaac still keeps skittles in his bottom left drawer."

For a second I forgot all about the paper, about my anxiety being here, about how all of this could blow up in my face…again. "Really?" I asked, glancing at the large desk in the front of the room, then back at Andy.

His eyes glinted wickedly, and he flashed a hand that sported a skittle between each finger tip.

"Hell, yes." I vacated my seat in favor of the treat and left Andy to what was likely to be a massacre. Sure enough, the lock was still busted and nestled within the bottom drawer was Mr. Isaac's guilty pleasure.

I swiped a handful, but instead of returning to my seat, I leaned back against the board and watched Andy read my attempt at scholastics. A red skittle found its way into my mouth, followed quickly by a yellow and a green. Back at the table, Andy stared thoughtfully at the pages and painted the damn things red. Between each bout of scribbles, he chewed on the end of the pen.

So that's still the same too.

His hair, his eyes, his habits…his mouth. Even as I had the dangerous thought, I couldn't stop myself. His mouth was definitely still the plush thing that plagued my dreams. Perhaps that was why I'd kissed him, to see if any of it was real, a test as it were. A test I'd failed miserably the second his body reacted to mine. In my defense, at eighteen, a warm anything could get my blood pumping, but nothing could have prepared me for the confident way he'd wrapped his arms around my neck and forced me to kiss him deeper. There was only one word for it—hungry. That was a feeling I was intimately familiar with.

"There."

My head snapped up from where I'd been studying the sugar melting in my hand. I popped the last few skittles and licked the sticky off as I made my way back to the table. The metal legs of the chair squeaked against the ground as I fell into it. "Alright, coach, how bad is it?"

Andy shook his head and laughed under his breath. "I'm 'coach' now, huh?"

I shrugged. "Would you rather I call you something else?"

"The technical term is tutor. Learn it, live it, love it," he said as he brandished the recapped pen at me. "And Andy will do just fine."

"Okay, Andy."

He stared at me for a long second without blinking, then adjusted his attention to the page.

I mirrored his gaze and almost choked at the sea of red. "Jesus Christ, Andy, what happened to taking it easy on me?"

"First off, pretty sure I said I wouldn't. Second, I thought the whole point of this was that you were tired of people going easy on you." He turned those green eyes on me and I swallowed. Andy had that kind of intense stare that dared you to contradict him. It dared you to do a lot of things.

"Yeah, okay. You're right."

The emerald challenge softened into a playful smirk. "I know."

"You know everything." The moment the words left my mouth, my heart stopped. I couldn't help it. They'd just…slipped free.

Andy only hesitated half a beat. "You make that sound like it's a bad thing. Also, you're going to want to wash your hands."

I frowned at him, but before I could do more, he reached out and snagged my wrist. I quickly added "not breathing" to the list of things I wasn't doing.

"Unless, of course, you wanna get busted for raiding the snack drawer."

I forced my gaze away from his sharp eyes and looked down at the captive hand. Sure enough, the melted skittles had left stains on my hand like a rainbow of freckles. My gaze slipped to Andy's firm grip, and the dusting of real freckles on his own hand.

As quickly as he'd snared it, he released my hand and started putting away his pen. "Don't be discouraged. The paper has promise." He gestured at the pages I didn't remember picking up. "Most of that is notes and suggestions for resource materials. Paper's due in a week. Should be plenty of time to clean it up."

"Yeah," I croaked out, because, again, had neglected to breathe.

"I, uh, could look at it again before you submit it." His gaze skittered over the table, but never actually met mine, which was probably for the best since I was pretty sure my face looked like the time I'd gotten beamed with a lacrosse stick.

Andy wants to see me again.

I rolled up the pages and stuffed them into my bag without really looking. "That would be great. I'd really like that," I said, my voice gaining strength.

Andy's roving gaze finally flicked up to meet mine and the small smile he'd given earlier grew to the one I remembered from our childhood, the one he'd given me when he'd declared we'd be best friends moments after meeting me. All too soon it was gone, lost as he shouldered his bag. And fuck, now I was going to bust my ass to make this the best paper I'd ever written, because I wanted to see it again.

Chapter 5

Four Years Ago

Andy

Euphoria coursed through my veins like a drug. Not that I'd ever done those. And euphoria was totally the right word. Right? Normally, I was better with words. Except for right now. Right now, all of my limbs sagged like overcooked noodles and my brain was a delirious pile of mush. I would have laughed if I'd had the energy. Which I didn't. And, fuck, wasn't that great? Euphoria was definitely the right word. That's all I was, a gooey mess of pure euphoria.

My ass twinged, and I winced against the unwelcome intrusion. Okay, maybe a little achy too, if I was being honest. Next time should probably use actual lube. A giggle bubbled in my chest. *Next time.* How could I already be thinking about a next time? My ass still burned, and I was one hundred percent positive I'd be sitting funny for days. Not to mention it had been way messier than I'd expected. But fuck if I cared. I *wanted* a next time. I wanted all the times. Until he did it, I didn't know how much I needed to be completely owned.

Mitch.

I just had sex with Mitch Hudson.

The bubbles of laughter threatened to boil right over into the world. I wanted to roll around like a lunatic, giggling my triumph. I, Anderson Gallagher, had had sex with Mitch Hudson, my best friend and the guy I'd been in love with who knew how long. And it had been incredible. I sighed through the laughter and pressed back into the warm body curled around me.

"Andy?" Mitch whispered into my hair, and hell if that didn't set off a fresh wave of goosebumps. "You awake?"

"Yeah," I squeaked out, then immediately bit my lip to prevent the laughter rioting inside me from spilling over. He snaked an arm around my waist and pulled me tight against him. Laying on the cold floor instead of a cushy bed sucked, but nothing could diminish my happiness at being snug in Mitch's embrace. The tiny part of me that had dared to believe Mitch could ever feel the same way burned a little brighter.

"Do you think I'll make the team?" Hearing the doubt and insecurity in his voice tore at my heart. Even though my back was to him, I knew he had a line between his brows like he got anytime he was worried, and I knew that smile I loved would be pointing the wrong direction. If I could have rolled over and kissed it back right ways, I would have, but his hold on me was too strong and not something I was willing to relinquish just yet.

"I know so," I said with all the confidence he couldn't seem to find.

He chuckled into my neck, the hot puffs of his breath warming the already flushed skin. "You know everything."

"You say that like it's a bad thing," I fired back. It was a familiar tease, and just one of the many things I loved about us. His thumb, already building calluses from hours of practice to try-out for said team, brushed across my lower abdomen and short-circuited my thoughts. The giddy high returned as my words abandoned me once more and I savored the caress.

Yeah, euphoria is definitely the right word.

Present Day

Andy

I stretched my legs out on grass warmed by the late afternoon sun. The light breeze kept the day pleasant and the clouds scuttling overhead offered intermittent shade. I let out a sigh and sank into the ground, letting it steal my tension as I looked down the steep hill to the field below where most of the lacrosse team was also enjoying the perfect day.

"Interesting choice of locale." Calvin's bag fell unceremoniously to the ground and sagged to the side, spilling an assorted collection of paint brushes and sketch pencils, not a pen or textbook to be seen. "Motherfucker," Calvin hissed, flopping to the earth and stuffing the rogue materials back in the bag.

I chuckled and reached into my satchel. "You know, there are these fancy things called cases you could use to keep your shit from trying to escape."

"Order is the ultimate enemy of a true artist. Chaos is my medium." Bag once again reassembled, he shoved it to the side where it threatened to have another episode. "You ignored my comment."

"Don't know what you're talking about."

"Uh-huh. How many times have I tried to get you to come up here with me?" The arched brow was over the top and pure Calvin. The sun highlighted his dark taupe skin, making him seem at once darker and brighter. He let out a dramatic breath and threw himself back, only to pop right back up again. "I see how it is. You help Mitch with one measly paper and suddenly it's okay to enjoy the view." He made a sweeping gesture to the flurry of activity below.

"It's a nice day," I countered, refusing to take the obvious bait. What may have started as one paper had quickly turned into three, including the English Lit one I was currently helping him with.

"I'm not begrudging you, the view—I mean day—is *very* nice," Calvin said as he returned to openly appreciating the players below.

"Do you have to leer like that?"

"If they didn't want to be looked at, then they shouldn't be running around half dressed, coated in delicious sparkling drops."

"It's hot."

He turned his lascivious grin on me and winked. "Yeah it is."

"Shut up, or I'm not giving you your pudding." I held out the stolen goods like they were the Holy Grail.

Calvin's eyes widened, and he made grabby hands. "Gimme gimme." He all but snatched the cup and fished out his own pilfered spoon from his rebellious satchel, humming with delight as he peeled back the lid. "I don't think I'll ever be able to reconcile the fact that *you* are a bit of a klepto."

I rolled my eyes and scooped a spoonful of chocolaty goodness. Filching treats had certainly been something I'd always been capable of, but it hadn't been until I learned Mitch loved the silly puddings that I'd started pilfering them from the cafeteria's secret stash. My gaze traveled across the players enjoying their friendly game. Mitch drew my attention like a magnet. Even from this distance, I could spot him no trouble. His smile threatened to split his face in two as he chased the ball only to steal it. Sweat dripped down his bare back, sliding past the defined dimples into his shorts. He'd changed over the last four years, from an awkwardly tall youth to this pinnacle of athletic perfection.

I adjusted my attention to my neglected pudding, but it couldn't stop my mind from wandering to places it shouldn't. Mitch didn't just look great, he felt it too. His hard body pressing me into the wall while his mouth conquered me with impunity, had been every dark desire I had come to life. The heat of him had threatened to burn me up, steal my senses…

It's just a game.

"Well, yeah. But wouldn't it be better if they played all their games like this?"

My head snapped up at Calvin's response.

"What? Look, you can say what you will, but we are *not* the only people who appreciate a good show around here," he added, waving his spoon at me.

I cleared my throat and banished all thoughts of what Mitch's body felt like against mine. "You think everyone is repressed."

"Aren't they? Just look at your boy." He gestured once more to the players below.

My gaze zeroed in on Mitch, his chest heaving from exertion and practically glowing with happiness. *So much for hating the team.*

"We at least know the shit he gets into and I doubt he's the only one, though maybe the only one with the balls to go for it. How are his balls these days, by the way? Still blue?"

My pudding went down the wrong way and I turned to disabuse Calvin of his belief that anything more than writing was happening between me and Mitch. Before I got the words out, though, he finished his thought.

"You still sticking to your not studying together?"

"Connor," I said as the reality of who he was talking about finally registered.

"Uh, yeah, *Connor*. Who the fuck else would I be talking about?" All the hoping in the world couldn't have stopped the light bulb from going off over his head. "Holy fucking mother of Christ, you boned Mitch."

"No, I didn't, and shut your trap before someone hears you," I snapped and tossed my half-eaten pudding aside.

Calvin's face scrunched with concern as he turned to face me. "Okay, fine, you're not boning him, but… Andy, are you sure it's a good idea to be spending so much time with him?"

I bristled at the implication. "We can be friends."

He searched my face a long minute before asking softly, "Can you?"

My gaze settled on Mitch once more, laughing, having fun, being someone else.

Calvin scooted closer until our shoulders were touching and leaned enough into me to offer comfort. "What do you think he would do if he saw us up here?"

"Probably come over." The words were out of my mouth before I could consider them.

"Yeah?"

I leaned back on my arms without taking my gaze off the figures below. "Yeah. I'm not sure why, but he seems to be trying to renew our friendship. And I... I kind of want to let him try." I glanced over at Calvin where he too stared riveted at the scene below. "Is that stupid?"

He shook his head and his gaze went distant. Calvin had his own demons to slay. One day I hoped more than anything that he'd get the knight in shining armor he deserved, someone to make all the pain bearable, but he'd have to let go of the past first. "It's not stupid, Andy. Just...be careful, okay?" he said, turning his suddenly dark gaze on me.

We looked at each other, then returned our focus to the players. I'd spent four years wrapping my heart in so many walls, it'd be a miracle if they ever crumbled. Connor hadn't even managed to peek over in the year and a half we'd been together. I didn't even know if *I* could break them at this point. But staring down at the first boy I'd ever fallen in love with, I knew, if anyone had the power to break me again, it was Mitchum Hudson.

"Well, today just got a lot fucking better."

The cheery comment startled me out of the dire thoughts, and I searched the area for its cause. Three more players had just joined the impromptu game, Benjamin Wallace Price IV at their helm. His shirt fell to the ground, and Calvin rubbed his hands with malicious glee.

"Do I need to leave?" I teased. Calvin made a grand show of rearranging himself in his pants and I laughed.

"I'm not saying you have to, but it might be in your best interest. Would hate to ruin those delicate sensibilities of yours."

I snorted. "And what do you think *he* would do if he saw us up here?"

"Stomp up here and throttle the living shit out of us. No question." Calvin winked and sat forward to watch the game with far more intensity than he'd started. I shook my head and followed suit. Calvin's obsession never ceased to amaze me. And of the two of us, he was actually the only one who knew how the damn game was played.

Chapter 6

Four Years Ago

Mitch

I just had sex with Andy. Like actual came-so-hard-I-saw-spots sex. With my best friend. Who was gay. On the floor. What. The. Fuck.

"Hey, Mitch?"

I swallowed past a sudden lump in my throat. "Yeah?"

"I'm glad it was you."

I blinked and stared at the back of his head, his red hair a darker Auburn in the dim lighting of the secret room. "What?"

"My first time, I'm glad it was with you."

I pulled back the arm that had been wrapped around him like he was actually made of fire like his hair suggested. "What?" I repeated, as if it would somehow change what he'd said.

He rolled onto his back and propped up on his elbows to look at me. His face twisted in confused concern that almost hid the wince that had passed over it when he'd shifted to a seated position.

Probably because his ass hurt. His virgin ass. Because Andy had never had sex before.

"Did you actually not hear me, or are you really going to make me say it again?"

"You've never done that before?" I wondered if it was possible to have an out-of-body experience while you were awake, because I sure as fuck didn't feel connected to mine at the moment.

Andy is a virgin… Well, not anymore. And I'd just… I hadn't even…

Andy cocked his head to the side, his green eyes darker than normal in the low light. "Uh, no. Hence the 'first time' comment. It's cool. I know you've been with…people." Girls. I'd been with girls. The slight pink that rarely stained Andy's cheeks made it clear that his thoughts mirrored mine. "I know my experience is basically nil compared to yours."

"But… You haven't been with anyone, like at all?" *Why am I struggling so hard with this? That's literally what he just said.* And yet, I couldn't let it go. I couldn't be Andy's first. I just couldn't. "Touching, kissing, anything?" I asked, my desperation growing.

He snorted, a rude sound that Andy seemed to have perfected for the sole goal of ratcheting up my rapidly increasing anxiety. "When would I have done that? We spend like every waking minute together. Pretty sure if I'd been sneaking around to hook up with guys you would've noticed." He shrugged. "Then again, if I had, then I wouldn't have needed to tell you I was gay." His teasing smile danced in his eyes like this was some kind of grand joke, one of the many we'd shared over the last two years. Except this shit wasn't funny, it wasn't funny at all. Andy had told me he was gay and instead of being a supportive best friend, I'd dragged him off and…*used* him. Sweet, *innocent* Andy, pure in his love of mischief and books… And I'd stolen it.

Shame boiled rancid hot in my belly like someone had shoved a white-hot poker into me.

Present Day

Mitch

"You're getting much better," Andy said, twirling his red pen between his fingers that thankfully had kissed the page far fewer times this go around. "Aside from a few grammatical errors, I'd say you have a solid B on your hands, maybe even an A."

I bit my lip and waited as he scribbled a quick note in the margin of the last page and highlighted a few more of the grammatical errors. "You really think so?" I couldn't even remember the last time I'd gotten an "A" without some bogus extra credit assignment that never actually happened.

"We've been through this. I know everything, remember?" The lid of his pen clicked in place. He slid the papers over to me, but didn't release them.

I glanced up at his serious face, so close I could see flecks of amber in his eyes.

"All joking aside, your grasp of the material is really good and your writing improvements are commendable." He blinked, his red lashes fanning briefly over his freckled cheeks. "I'm impressed, Mitch. You've worked really hard. You should be proud of yourself."

My heart swelled at the generous compliment. I didn't realize how much I missed someone building me up, helping me to be better for myself and no one else.

Maybe he can forgive me, maybe I can have my friend back.

The distance between us shrank as if gravity itself was pulling us together. Deep-seated longing slowly worked its way out until it filled every cell. I missed my best friend, my companion and partner in crime. I missed Andy, missed his laugh and wit, missed his spark and mischief. His warm breath fell from parted lips and his eyelids fluttered. Guilt at how I'd treated him back then threaded beneath the ache of longing.

Whatever it takes, I'll get him back.

His breath hitched, and the tip of his tongue traveled over his lips. My gaze followed its path while my mind went to the one place it shouldn't. I remembered every microsecond of kissing Andy. The way his lips had molded against mine, the way his tongue had danced and played, the hunger that seemed to radiate off of him. I wasn't supposed to like it, wasn't supposed to want it. But I did. I wanted it so fucking much it hurt.

I wasn't even sure I was breathing anymore as the space between us dwindled to millimeters. Suddenly, Andy jolted back as if he'd been electrocuted and the fog wrapped around my brain fell. I sat back, putting more distance between us, my heart pounding furiously against my ribs. My gaze darted over to the door and I swallowed. What was I thinking? What if someone had walked in? That'd be a fine way to earn Andy's forgiveness. My fingers clawed into the paper and I dragged it closer.

Beside me, I felt as much as saw Andy's walls go up. He put away his pen with stiff hands and refused to look back over at me. "Like I was saying, keep up the good work."

Bile crawled up my throat at the familiar, flat encouragement. How many times had the coach said the same thing, only to demand more from me? There was no such thing as enough, not when there was more to give. And there always was.

I pushed my chair back and reached for my bag so I could put the paper away. "Thanks again for all the help." I looked down at his red hair and struggled to find the words that could make this better, some way to restore the fleeting moment of real friendship.

He stiffened as if he could feel my gaze on him and his hand hovered inside his bag. He slowly withdrew it and a thin book. "This should help." He stared at the book, then stood. Head down, he offered me what turned out to be a thesaurus.

My fingers closed around the worn binding, and his gaze finally rose to meet mine.

"I circled a few words that you over use. This should offer some alternatives. If…" He paused and licked his lips like he had earlier, "if you have any questions…let me know?" The hint of question snagged my attention.

I searched his face, not sure if I understood what was happening. Had Andy just given me…a peace offering? Even after I'd literally just royally screwed up? "Yeah, I'll do that." My voice came out unexpectedly thick, but I couldn't have cared less as the corners of his mouth ticked up in a smile and he released the book.

"You'll tell me how it goes?" he asked, stuffing his hands into his pockets.

I nodded, not trusting any actual words in the wake of the hope that surged through me like a tidal wave. Andy was actually going to give me a chance to make things right. All I had to do was not fuck it up. Again.

Andy

The bookstore door shut behind me with a tinkling of bells. I stroked the soft leather of my bag, now near to bursting with my latest acquisitions. The books brought with them their own sense of joy, yet despite the hours I'd devoted to getting lost among the shelves filled with other realities, my own continued to haunt me. More specifically, the reality in which I was talking to Mitch again. I didn't expect this sudden renewal of friendship to last, but a rebellious part of me dared to dream, and no matter how deep I shoved the blind hope, it just kept coming back, relentless, undeniable, determined…

We're studying, that's all, nothing more. Fall training will start in earnest and this sudden desire to improve his grades will be pushed aside.

I shook my head and focused on the ground moving beneath my feet. Three steps away from the only decent bookstore in the sad little town of Hylestad, someone yanked me off the street. Being short didn't bother me most days, but being manhandled was another story altogether.

My feet skidded over the gritty pavement, incapable of finding purchase. Rays of sunshine cut sharp swaths of light in the dim alley. My bag thudded heavily against the brick wall now pressing into my back. A shout filled my lungs but never found voice as a mouth closed over mine. Instant recognition poured through me, washing the fight away. Half a heartbeat is all it took to decide. I slipped into the easy familiarity of the demanding mouth, tasting and teasing with a playfulness perfected with practice.

His lips pulled on mine as he dragged out a languid kiss that we could never enjoy freely in the open. "Mm, seems like someone misses me."

"In your dreams, Connor," I quipped, my gaze flicking to his storm blue eyes.

He snickered a low laugh and pressed me more firmly into the wall. "And what do you know of my dreams?"

Rather than answer, I kissed him again, indulging in the simplicity of the moment and doing my damnedest to let go of the stress from moments before. Our tongues tangled together as I took ownership of the kiss and dragged a needy moan out of him. Connor's buttons had always been easy to push. They were right on the surface. He angled forward and my fingers scraped over his hard-won abs. Calvin wasn't the only one with a type. I splayed my hand over the defined muscles and felt Connor's stomach flex in anticipation.

What is it about athletes? These long, lean bodies. Muscles for days...

My hand itched to explore, but before it could go anywhere, thoughts of another athlete intruded on my appreciation of Connor's eager body. Mitch's muscles weren't all that different, except he was taller, and well, better. I still burned at the memory of him pressing me into the wall, using his whole body to hold me there while he completely owned me, like only he could, like he always had...

Like he always will.

I sucked in a breath and pulled away from the bad decision already in full swing.

"What's the matter?" Connor asked as he endeavored to tempt me with another kiss. "Change your mind again already?"

"Nothing to change. We're not getting back together," I said with all the monotone I could muster. I may not understand why Mitch was suddenly so eager to spend time together, but I did know it wasn't right to take out my frustrations on Connor. No one deserved to be used like that.

He made a rude sound in his throat. "Come on, Gallagher. Doesn't mean we can't still have a little fun now and then. Right?" His hands slid provocatively around my waist, and for a tiny moment, I was genuinely tempted. "That *is* how this whole thing started, remember?" He tipped my nose with his own, his breathing as husky as his words, while his hard-on pressed into my stomach.

I quirked a smile at him. "I remember. Which is exactly why this stops here." I flattened my hand on his chest and pushed. His crestfallen look might have been comical if it also hadn't been so childishly affected, like someone had stolen his candy.

Mitch would never look at me like that.

He huffed and spun to lean against the same wall as me. "Suit yourself, but don't pretend you don't miss me."

"Missing you and *missing* you aren't quite the same. Or are you fishing?" I teased. As remarkable as it was, some days, Connor's insecurities seemed to run deeper than mine.

"Shut your face. I had a rough day. So sue me for wanting a pick me up."

I sighed and didn't say what I'd said a million times before—that right there was why we didn't work. I didn't want to be somebody's pick me up to use only when they were feeling blue. We may go to school with a clusterfuck of bigots, but I deserved to be happy, to be appreciated for who I was, to have a companion, a friend and a lover.

Someone like Mitch.

I growled to myself and adjusted the strap threatening to slip off my shoulders. Mitch wanting help with classes wasn't the same and it never would be.

"Don't get your panties in a twist," Connor griped. "Fuck, you're so serious all the time. Learn to live a little."

"Like you?"

He flashed an obnoxious grin. "Yeah, like me. What do you have in there today?" he asked, poking into my satchel like the nosy ass he was.

"Books."

"Surprise, surprise." He rolled his eyes and withdrew his questing hand.

"About murder."

"Frankly, I don't give a damn if that was a threat or a genre. I keep telling you, they keep the juicy stuff in the back."

"And I keep telling you, I have no interest in reading smut." Especially since the store hadn't gotten any new stuff in ages. Of course, Connor didn't need to know that I'd found the horde of erotica sequestered in the back behind a velvet current three years ago, then promptly devoured every page.

"Your loss. Anyway…" He danced his fingers along my thigh, bringing them perilously closer to my groin. "You sure I can't persuade you?"

I gently, but firmly, grabbed his hand and repositioned it over his own crotch. "Sorry, but you'll have to continue with…self-study."

He unsurprisingly groped himself and leered back. "We'll see. You'll come around eventually. And when you do—"

"I will have clearly lost my mind and should be committed."

He barked out a laugh and pushed his long frame off the wall, abandoning his lewd show. "See you around, Gallagher." He took another step closer to the mouth of the alley, winked, then was gone.

I stayed in the shadows awhile longer and continued to fight with myself. Renewing a friendship with Mitch was likely an even greater act of insanity than renewing a relationship with Connor. And yet, here I was, bound and determined to see if it would work. Except, all my efforts to protect myself from getting hurt again were already suffering heavy losses. The near-kiss the other day was proof of that. I'd just have to make my walls thicker, build them higher, whatever it to took to protect my heart from the one person guaranteed to break it. I wouldn't survive a second time.

My groan bounced back at me in the narrow space and I rested my head against the wall as I grappled with the insurmountable task of not falling for Mitchum Hudson…again.

Chapter 7

Four Years Ago

Mitch

It didn't take long for Andy to fall asleep. My sleep, however, remained elusive, not that I could have closed my eyes if I wanted to. As it was, it took everything I had not to ralph on the floor. Still might have, if I hadn't been so worried about the sound of my dry heaves waking him up. I devoted all my energy to keeping my stomach under control until I was positive he was solidly out.

Once I was confident he wouldn't wake if I moved, I shifted to do just that. Before I could though, he grabbed my arm and wrapped it around his torso, then preceded to use me like a human blanket. Acid boiled in my stomach while pain stung sharply behind my eyes. He was so small, so fragile. I was his best friend. I was supposed to protect him, not...what I'd done.

Eventually, his hold on me relaxed enough that I could remove my arm. I stared at it for a long minute as if it somehow held the secret to go back in time and undo this horrible mess I'd made. It didn't. Nothing could undo what I'd done. I shook it out and got dressed as quietly as I could. Every cell in my body screamed at me to just go, don't look back, walk away while I still could, while there was still a chance of fixing this, or better yet, wake him up, make sure we were on the same page or at least in the same book. I did neither. Instead, I leaned against the wall and slid down to the floor, my gaze riveted on the image of shattered innocence before me. I'd stay just a minute to gather my thoughts and then I'd go.

Except I didn't.

I sat and watched Andy sleep on that hard floor in a cold room that almost no one knew existed. I remained perfectly still as goosebumps roved across his flesh, crawling over him like a thousand tiny insects. Didn't blink when he curled in tighter on himself to ward off the chill. I just sat there and watched, while a hollowness spread throughout my chest. With each second that ticked by, it found and devoured every bright spot of light inside me. All the joy I'd had at the beginning of the night died a slow and painful death.

By the time I got up, I was positive there wasn't an ounce of feeling left in me. I pushed the giant portrait away from the wall and stared into a hallway as bleak as my soul. Did monsters even have souls? Because that's what I was now, a monster. Only a monster could betray their best friend in this entire world's trust like I had. My stomach heaved, and I choked on bile. I sprinted as fast as my feet would carry me to the nearest bathroom.

The stall door bounced on its hinges, its hollow echo as it smacked its neighbor ringing through the room. Pain radiated through my knees as I crashed to the ground and threw up the last two years. Every extra pudding we'd ever stolen, every filched sweet from a teacher's desk, every moment of laughter over a shared summer memory. All of it, gone, and I only had myself to blame.

Present day

Mitch

I swallowed my anxiety as Professor Garza pulled out a manila envelope. He considered me a moment, his brown eyes sharp and scrutinizing, before stepping around the desk that separated us. I willed myself not to assume the worst, but considering everyone else had gotten their grades the normal way, I wasn't doing well. He held out the folder, and I took it with a miraculously steady hand. I immediately flipped it over, only to find the adhesive gluing it shut.

"Um… Can I ask why it's sealed?"

He perched on the edge of his desk, his fingers curling over the top, and smiled. "Figured you might like to share the results with Anderson."

My face went cold as all the blood immediately vacated it. "Why would I want to do that?" I asked, aiming for calm and missing it by a mile.

"I'd recognize his handiwork anywhere."

The desk scraped loudly against the floor as I lurched out of it. "He didn't write it. I swear he didn't. He would never do that. Andy-"

"Is tutoring you," Garza interrupted. "I'm glad. I wish I could convince him to tutor more of my students."

"You…you don't think he wrote it for me?" I floundered, put off by his response.

Garza's mouth twisted into a frown. "Forget the fact that Anderson would never do such a thing, I'm devout in my belief that your own morals wouldn't allow it even if he had offered. You put in the work and the results show that. I'm simply suggesting that Anderson might appreciate sharing in your victory is all."

"Oh, um, okay," I stammered and clutched the folder to my chest. "So, it wasn't bad?"

"Not in the least. One of the best in your class, actually."

A smile tugged at my mouth as I glanced down at the golden envelope. *One of the best?*

"Go on, get out of here." Garza glanced up at the clock. "He should be getting out of Nolan's class pretty soon. He'll probably welcome a good diversion after that," he added with a half-smile.

I did a double take. Had Garza really just knocked one of the other professors? Sure, Nolan was a total tool, but weren't they all supposed to be unified or some shit?

In answer to my unasked question, Garza said, "Being part of the faculty doesn't automatically make us all friends. He is a bit of a fresa."

I frowned at the unusual term while Garza walked back around his desk. In the hall, boys were already pouring out of their last classes and filling the air with excited chatter.

Garza settled back in his chair and resumed grading another class's assignments. After a moment, he glanced back up. "What are you still doing here? If you don't hurry, you'll miss him." He smiled ruefully as I carefully slipped the envelope in my bag and rushed into the crowd outside. I only made it as far as the next junction when a familiar voice called me up short.

"Hud-son." Even dropped to a low bass, the voice and the exaggerated extension of my name carried easily in the vaulted hall. I squeezed my eyes shut and sent up a silent prayer that he was on his own as I turned to address its owner.

"Hey Brian," I said with practiced calm. Despite my hope, he was flanked by Nate and John, his dark brown skin contrasting with their lighter tan.

"Where are you off to in such a hurry?" he asked as he and the others formed a half circle around me.

I nodded to Nate and fist-bumped Brian and John. "Nowhere special."

"Good, then you can come with us. We were gonna head into town."

Just then, I spied a familiar satchel over-burdened with books. "Actually…uh…" I took a step back, breaking their circle. "There was something I wanted to do." My fingers tightened around the strap of my bag while anxiety threatened to turn me into a stammering idiot.

Nate elbowed Brian and smiled crookedly. "Something or some*one*."

"Maybe a certain redhead?" John added.

I groaned inwardly, but was half a second away from letting them assume whatever they wanted, as long as it got me out of this before Andy vanished altogether. Then Brian's gaze shifted behind me.

"Oh shit, it's Nolan. Scatter." Just like that, I was free to pursue the object of my quest as all four of us dispersed without another word.

By sheer dumb luck, I caught up to Andy just as he reached the south exit. His eyebrows raised in surprise at my sudden appearance, and he glanced behind me. He seemed to do that a lot when other people were around. For once, I was with him. I didn't want to share this with anyone else.

"Do you have a minute?"

"What for?" His gaze slid past me to triple check the hallway.

"I got my results for the lit paper."

His green eyes snapped back to me, fever bright. "And?"

I bit my lip. "I haven't looked at it yet, but Garza said it was good." I ran a hand over my bag and thought of the sealed envelope within. "He thought you might like to find out with me since you helped me with it."

Andy made a low, strangled sound deep in his throat. "Well, come on." He grabbed my wrist and started off down the nearest hallway. A hallway that would conveniently lead us to the portrait of Ulwich.

Andy

The lights were still struggling to brighten when I reached for Mitch's bag. I got as far as flipping it open before he danced back with a laugh.

"Eager much?"

"Don't pretend like you're not. Quit with the stalling." I made a come-on gesture with my hand and he laughed again.

"Yeah, you're right. I thought the worst when he asked me to come back after my last class to pick it up." He reached into the bag and pulled out a manila envelope, its seal unbroken.

"You really haven't seen yet?" I asked in wonder.

"Nope. I have to say, when Garza said you'd be just as eager to know, I didn't really believe him." He slipped a finger between the fold and tossed me a smirk. "Guess I was wrong."

"You planning to open it at all?" I deadpanned.

He dropped his gaze back to the folio. "Yeah. Okay. Yeah, I am," he said, but rather than continue peeling the adhesive apart, he hesitated, his teeth sinking into his bottom lip. Then it hit me. He was nervous.

I stepped up to him and placed a hand on his forearm. "Hey, there's nothing to be worried about. You did really well. Garza even said so."

He nodded and licked his lips, then finally opened the envelope. I waited with bated breath as he withdrew the pristine white pages stapled together. The moment the pages were free, Mitch sucked in a breath. Impatience tore at me. From my angle, all I could make out was the red circle around the grade. Finally, his gaze lifted from the page and latched onto mine.

"I did it," he whispered with awe. "You were right. I actually did it." His fingers tightened around the pages. I didn't even need to see the grade anymore, the insanely bright smile on his face was reward enough. "Fuck, Andy, I did it." He barked a laugh and released the paper to flutter to the ground and surged forward, his hands coming to rest on my face.

I went stock still as his lips pressed against mine. My entire brain short-circuited, and I forgot how to move or even blink. My body thrummed like a tuning fork and the air froze in my lungs.

As suddenly as he'd caught me, Mitch pulled away. "Shit. I'm sorry. I just...got caught up. I didn't... I mean..." he stammered along while he rubbed the back of his neck and valiantly failed at looking like anything other than an awkward goose.

I forced my eyes to close and reopen, the shock of what had just happened still playing through me. Without my brain to interfere, all sorts of forbidden thoughts were lighting up with abandon. "It's...fine," I said awkwardly, the words thick in my mouth as I reminded my tongue how to speak.

He gave me a sheepish look, then did what Mitch did best—he ignored what had just happened. "An 'A', Andy. An honest to goodness 'A'. Thank you."

I blinked more naturally this time and fought to refortify the walls he'd casually traipsed past. "You're welcome, but you really did most of the work."

"You're being generous, but thanks anyway." He scooped up the neglected pages and dusted them off, before reverently replacing them in the envelope. Then he bit his lip again and flicked his gaze back at where I was still standing like a shell-shocked lump. His hazel eyes caught the yellow glow of the ancient lights overhead. "We should celebrate."

A familiar wariness snaked through my veins. "What did you have in mind?"

"Something for old time's sake? A prank?" he suggested tentatively. Like the kiss, the idea hit me out of nowhere. But maybe...maybe the answer to all of this wasn't guarding against everything. Just because Mitch could never feel about me the way I'd once felt about him didn't mean we couldn't have a little fun, as Connor put it.

Why shouldn't I enjoy this?

"A prank…could be fun," I conceded. His latest smile completely trumped the previous one and my own begged to be set free. "Who did you have in mind?"

"What would you say to Nolan?"

My smile finally broke free and the corners of my lips curled up in a wicked grin. "I'd say I have an idea."

Chapter 8

Andy

I walked down the hall and did my best not to look like I was up to no good. Luckily, filching art supplies was way less suspect than acquiring a dozen *live* frogs. By the time I reached the art room, I'd only passed two staff members and a handful of students, none of which had spared me a second glance.

After a quick survey of the otherwise empty hall, I slipped inside, careful to make sure the door shut quietly. Calvin's instructions had been remarkably succinct, and I spotted my destination almost immediately. I crossed the vacant room to the tall black cabinet on the far side and let out a sigh of relief to find it unlocked. Calvin had said it would be, just like he'd said the class would be outside working on blending techniques today, but I'd brought supplies just in case he'd been mistaken. Not that I was confident in my lock picking abilities. It had been a long while. Besides, picking locks had always been Mitch's forte.

Giddiness bubbled inside of me. We were doing a prank together. That he'd followed along with my schemes since that first day I'd nearly bowled over him six years ago without so much as lifting an eyebrow had been one of my absolute favorite things about our friendship. About him. Understandably, once I had a partner in crime, the pranks only got more elaborate, hence the epic Dust Frog Caper. Who knows how we would have topped that one if we hadn't broken up.

I paused. "Broken up" made it sound like we'd been dating. Much as my heart at the time would have loved that, I understood now that had never been in the cards nor would it ever be. Mitch might be curious, but he was most definitely straight. All it took was one look at him and his girlfriend, Trixie, with her garish red hair trying to eat each other's faces to confirm the belief. Not that I would ever tell Mitch that I'd stumbled across them in town last term or that I'd stood frozen and watched them until his team-mates called him away.

I shook my head clear of the awful memory, then checked the clock to make sure I still had plenty of time. Again, Calvin had said they'd be out most of the period, but there was no sense in dawdling. I undid the straps on my satchel, then removed the books sitting on top to reveal the empty box beneath. It had been significantly harder than I'd expected to find a container big enough to hold the art supplies, but small enough to fit in my bag without being conspicuous.

Smirking at my genius, I set the books down and opened the cabinet wide. Toward the back, tucked away in a dust filled corner, were the promised tubes of paint. I plucked one out to inspect, leaving a perfect ring of dust in its wake. *Lamp Black Acrylic*. Calvin was positive no one would miss it as his mentor and the head art professor, Jankowski, abhorred what was apparently a *very* bad batch. I debated taking all of them, but given the size of the containers, I opted to only take three. Besides, I figured a few missing tubes were easier to explain than all of them vanishing.

I wiped my hands free of the dust on some nearby painter's cloth, then replaced the books and closed the cabinet. Satisfied with my handiwork, I sauntered out of the room, unable to keep my grin to myself.

"Well, well, well. What do we have here?"

I froze mid-step on my way back to chemistry. The paint hidden in my bag felt like it might as well have been a beacon broadcasting my guilt to the entire school. I swallowed down the burst of nerves and turned to face my accuser, then promptly relaxed. "Connor. Aren't you supposed to be in class?"

His sandy blond eyebrows lifted. "Aren't you?" I reflexively clutched the strap of my satchel and his gaze darted to the open straps—because, of course, I'd forgotten to synch them. "What's in the bag, Gallagher?"

"None of your business." I could have bitten my tongue clean off. Why hadn't I just said books?

"Uh-huh." He crossed his arms, accentuating his wide shoulders and muscular biceps that I definitely wasn't noticing…or comparing to Mitch's. Connor tilted his head toward the art room, where the door hadn't closed completely.

I could have hissed with annoyance. Since when did I make such rookie mistakes? Was I really *that* out of practice?

"What were you doing in the art room?"

"Since when do you care about what I do?" I snapped.

Connor nodded to himself and stuffed one of his hands in his pocket as he walked up to me. "That's fair."

I tightened my hold on the bag as he lifted his free hand, fully prepared to defend it. Except he didn't reach for the satchel. He lightly held my chin, lifting it slightly while his thumb rubbed beneath my mouth. I swallowed thickly. "W-what are you doing?"

His gaze lifted from my parted lips. "I'm talking to you, Andy. I'm paying attention. Wasn't that one of the reasons you said we didn't work?"

I licked my lips and glanced behind him, relieved to see we were still alone. But that wouldn't last. "This isn't really the place for this."

"I know," he said with a sigh, releasing his tentative hold. "Shame really. You don't deserve to be anyone's secret."

My breath caught and my eyes began to sting. I dropped my focus to the floor, unable to continue meeting his soft gaze. What was all this about? Did he know about Mitch?

"I'm sorry. I didn't mean to upset you." He fisted the hand that had been holding my face, then shoved it in his other pocket. "This place, it sucks the decency out of you, turns you into someone you never wanted to be. I know we had our issues, but it wasn't all bad, right?"

I lifted my head sharply. "Of course not."

Connor stepped closer and dropped his voice to a whisper. "I still believe we could be good together. Give us another chance. I'll show you."

To my shame, I considered the proposal. He wasn't wrong. We *could* be really good together. We got along well enough. Had enough differences to keep things interesting. But... But we'd both be sacrificing part of ourselves to make it work. I knew that, even if Connor didn't. Agreeing would only hurt us both in the long run.

I took a step back, determined to be strong. "No, Connor." Guilt stabbed my heart at the hurt that flashed in his eyes. "I appreciate what you're saying, I really do, and... And you're not wrong. But it was more than the not talking. You know that."

"We could at least try. I miss you."

His plea tore at my heart. I'd never been wrapped up in Connor the way I'd been with Mitch, but I did care for him. Which was why I had to remain firm. Cutting ties now was the right thing to do—for both of us. I may not deserve to be anyone's secret, but neither did he. One day, Connor would find someone who complimented him and embraced *all* the things that made him an incredible person. And if I was being honest with myself, it broke my heart a little to admit that would never be me.

Mitch

I wiped my hands on my khakis and stepped into the locker room. Thankfully, the rest of the team wasn't here…yet. They'd be along eventually, but Coach Santinelli had asked to speak with me privately. I didn't have to be Andy-level smart to know that wasn't a good thing.

The empty rows of lockers and benches seemed to pass silent judgment on me as I crossed the room, as if they knew all my dirty secrets. For all of its emptiness, it was full to the brim with memories…most unpleasant. There was the bench I'd been standing by when I'd gotten pantsed on my first official day as part of the team. Laughter had echoed off the walls until it seemed like it would break right through the concrete. That was the locker we'd shoved a naked angry Teri into. He'd quit the team a week later. My steps faltered when I passed the spot where'd I'd officially learned what tea-bagging was. For a school full of elitist homophobes, they had some questionable ideas about "fun".

I dried my sweaty palms again before reaching up to knock on the coach's office door. The glass panel was frosted, so I couldn't tell much besides that at least one person was inside. The knock felt overly loud without the loud buzz of the team to fill the silence.

"Come in!"

I slowly opened the door, doing my best to hide my silent hope that the purpose of this meeting was to kick me from the team. "You wanted to see me, Coach?"

Coach Santinelli glanced up from what looked like a new playbook. His sandy complexion had weathered with time and too much sun into something more like leather than skin. He still had a full head of dark hair that he kept short, but if you looked closely, you could make out the rebellious silver strands. The pictures he kept on his desk showed that he'd once been young and attractive. But it was hard to reconcile the youthful smile of the man in the photos with the stern hard ass before me. "Hudson. Come in. Have a seat."

Coach had always been more on the...blunt side, and didn't like repeating himself. I quickly moved to occupy the seat across from him. Despite the plush cushion, I didn't dare get comfortable.

He set his pen down and rested his forearms on the desk while he stared at me intently. "Do you know why I've asked you here today?"

I had a pretty good idea, but past interactions with Coach had taught me the hard way to never supply an answer first. My leg started to bounce and I willed it still. After the silence dragged on for an uncomfortable amount of time, he leaned back and laced his fingers over his stomach.

"Your performance these last few weeks has left a lot to be desired. Care to explain yourself?" Despite the obvious question, I knew better than to mistake it for one.

"I—" My voice hitched. I cleared my throat and sat up straighter. "I've been working on building my grades up." While it had technically only been the one, I wanted to be clear that I cared about all of them.

Coach snorted and pushed out of his chair. "The grades will be taken care of." He waved a dismissive hand as he walked toward the most prominent picture on the wall—Class of '87 Lacrosse Team.

I bristled. Thankfully, his back was to me, otherwise I'd likely still be doing laps when the rest of the team showed up later in the afternoon. Before I could come up with a response, Coach was talking again.

"You have promise, Hudson, like your father."

My gaze cut toward the picture that I'd memorized by heart. I didn't have to see it clearly to make out my dad in his uniform, only a few people down from Santinelli himself. When I'd learned they'd not only gone to school together, but played together as well, I'd been excited, eager to hear the stories. How naïve I'd been.

Coach spun around, his hands clasped behind his back. "I'd hate to see you waste yours the way he did." Coach's lip curled up in a sneer like it did anytime he talked about my dad, which thankfully had turned out to be hardly ever. To say they'd been rivals would have been putting it nicely. Given how much Coach Santinelli clearly hated my dad, it was a wonder I'd ever made the team in the first place. Most days, I wished I hadn't.

I thought about Andy and how we were plotting a fresh prank for the first time in years. That shot of joy buoyed me enough to moderate my response. "I won't, sir. I know the team is counting on me."

"You're damn right they're counting on you." He smacked the flat of his palm on the desk so hard I gave an involuntary jump. "The culmination of the team's efforts will be this spring. And your future isn't the only one riding on getting a sport's scholarship."

I swallowed and dropped my gaze to the floor. This was it. He was going to order me not to study anymore. He'd have my grades adjusted enough to pass, but not enough to raise suspicions with any school interested in taking me on. The prank with Andy could very well be the last time we'd get to hang out, maybe ever. If I'd known four years ago that lacrosse would consume every aspect of my life, whether I wanted it to or not, I never would have tried out for the team.

"Well, what do you have to say for yourself? Can we count on you to carry your weight?" Santinelli demanded to know.

Anger spiked through me and I balled fists in my lap. It wasn't just *my* weight he wanted me to carry; it was the whole fucking team's. We had some damn good players, but they weren't me. Without me, they didn't have a prayer of winning the championship in the spring, let alone qualifying. They knew it. Coach knew. And most importantly, *I* knew it.

I launched out of my seat, practically vibrating with years of pent up anger. This was too much pressure, it always had been, and I was fucking done. If Santinelli kicked me off the team and I no longer had a sports scholarship to fall back on, then so be it.

"What do you think you're doing?" Coach snapped, his glower as fierce as ever. And I... Didn't. Give. A fuck.

"If it's all the same to you, Coach, I think I'll keep studying. There won't be a need to...'take care of' my grades. I'll take care of them myself." I caught his gaze, his deep brown eyes all but blazing with fury at my outburst, and I refused to backdown. "Was there anything else?" I waited a beat before adding, "Coach."

His nostrils flared while his face darkened to the purple side of crimson. "You've just won yourself laps."

"How many?" I asked, crossing my arms over my chest.

"Until I tell you to stop. Now get the hell out of my office, Hudson!"

"Gladly, sir." I turned on my heel and marched out the way I'd come, letting the metal door slam shut behind me.

"Make that double time!" Coach Santelli yelled after me.

I ripped open my locker, which, coincidentally, had also been my dad's. His initials scored into the back seemed to mock me as I traded out my school uniform for practice gear. I snarled at them before slamming the door shut again. It was probably a good thing he wasn't around anymore to see me fuck up my life. After that little display, Coach would likely be making my days a living hell until I left this school once and for all. Which meant I needed to make the most out of this prank with Andy. I might never get another shot.

Chapter 9

Mitch

The light of the half-moon shone through the nearby window, completely washing Andy out. Even his outrageously auburn hair was muted in the dim light. He shook his hands like they were wet and paced in a five-foot area. I laughed to myself. How many times had I seen him do that? Too many to count.

"Nervous?" I asked, walking the rest of the way to him.

"Mitch!" he hissed and promptly smacked me in the chest.

"Ow."

"Why do you always have to sneak up on me?" Despite the accusing question, his face erupted in a grin that made his eyes dance. "Mitch." The way he said it made it sound like it wasn't his first attempt to get my attention.

"Yeah?"

"You ready?"

"Depends. Were you able to get some?"

An evil grin spread across his face as he held up three tubes of black paint.

I smiled in return. I was probably one of two people in the entire school who knew how devious Andy could be.

"Come on, let's go." His urgent whisper had excitement fizzing inside of me like a shaken soda, and if the way his grin kept popping out was any judge, he felt the same.

We sprinted silently through the empty halls like a pair of shadows. At last, our destination loomed before us. As I knelt down level with the doorknob, a sudden bout of giggles hit Andy. I shook my head. Some things never changed.

I took out a bobby pin I'd acquired from my time with Trixie and set to work on the lock. Andy gave a quiet snort, and I glanced up at him. He had his eyebrows raised in silent judgment, knowing damn well where the pin had come from. I gave him a look and returned to my task while he tried to quell his amusement. The door made a soft click. We glanced down each passageway, then slipped inside.

"Okay. Where do we start first?" Andy asked in a hushed whisper as I carefully closed the door.

"Everything Nolan touches all the time, for sure."

"Definitely the eraser then. I'd say the marker too, but there's no way to coat it without it getting on everything else and ruining the surprise," he added as he liberally applied a layer of paint to the dark handle of the board eraser, careful not to get any on himself.

I caught the tube he lobbed at me. "And of course, it can only be black things."

"Hey, you agreed on the color."

"I'm just poking at you," I whispered in his ear as I walked past him. He made a face at me and stuck out his tongue. I chuckled to myself and set about finding several items to doctor as well. Out of the corner of my eye, I saw Andy shift to the wall full of windows, silently coating pretty much every dark item he could find. "You sure it won't dry?" I asked for probably the tenth time.

He scowled at me. "Calvin said this shit takes days to stop being tacky."

I laughed quietly and stepped back to admire our handiwork. You totally couldn't tell. "Can you think of anything else?" I asked aloud.

He stood a moment, holding the nearly empty third bottle up as he considered the room. I watched him mentally tick off all the likely items we'd already covered, as well as the less likely. He chewed on his lip, still musing when inspiration suddenly lit his face. "I've got it!" he shout-whispered. He stepped back and bumped Nolan's notoriously over-stuffed bookcase. Andy froze as the giant structure teetered behind him.

Faster than what I would have thought possible, I reached out and snatched him out of harm's way. I clutched him to my chest as several large books tumbled to the ground right where he'd been standing. The first book made a loud smack as it landed on the floor, while those that collided after were more muffled. If one of those had hit him…

Time seemed to stretch around us as we waited for the noise to be investigated. Andy was so close I could feel his heart beating against my chest. I looked down at him and had to resist the urge to crook a finger under his chin and tilt his head up. In my mind's eye, I did it anyway.

My heart slowed as I looked into eyes the color of summer framed by golden red lashes. I forgot how to breathe as my gaze rested on his mouth. Andy had the softest lips I'd ever tasted. They parted slightly, an invitation I gladly took. He wrapped his arms around my neck and I sighed into him, longing for more. It was moments like this, with him completely cocooned in my embrace, that I remembered how much shorter than me he was. The half a foot difference didn't mean much as I tightened my grip around his waist, fully prepared to lift him so he could wrap his legs around me.

"I don't think anyone is coming, do you?" His question effectively broke the spell, and I crashed back to reality, where the only heart beating furiously was mine.

"I think you're right," I said, releasing him. He stepped over to the fallen books and held up a large tomb that could have easily snapped his neck.

"You okay?" I asked, struggling to keep my sudden anxiety at bay. None of our pranks had ever risked actually hurting one of us.

"Only thanks to you," he responded with a smirk, then promptly smacked me with the book.

We made quick work of righting the room. By the time we were done, there wasn't a trace we'd ever been there. Unless, of course, you touched something black.

"I think that's it," I declared, pleased as punch with what we'd accomplished *and* that no one had investigated the ruckus.

"Wait," he said, pulling me up short.

"What?"

"One more thing." He took back out the remaining paint.

"We've gotten everything. What else is left?"

"I wanna get the chair." His eyes glittered maliciously in the moon's light spilling through the wall of windows.

This is why we're best friends. Imp.

"Okay, but don't paint the whole seat. I have an idea."

I laughed as I fell to the floor in the secret room, too wired to even try to go to bed. Mercifully, Andy was of the same mind. He was an even worse giddy mess than when the evening had started.

I tried not to think about how close it had come to being a terrible night instead of the incredible fun it had been.

"I thought for sure our goose was cooked when you bumped that shelf."

Andy laughed as he joined me on the floor. "I forgot you use all those antiquated phrases," he said, stretching out and chuckling to himself.

"What's wrong with my phrases?"

"Come on. 'Our goose was cooked'? What era are you from?" he teased, then promptly disintegrated into giggles. "Oh god," he gasped between fits, "I can't remember the last time I pulled off a successful prank." He let out a huge sigh and relaxed into the floor. I could.

I angled my body so I was on my side, facing him. He looked at me from his back, his eyes still bright, with a smile playing at the corners of his mouth. I loved him like this: carefree and relaxed, remembering there was more to life than studying and good grades.

He ran his hands over his face and flopped them to the ground. "I feel high. Don't you feel high?" It was quite the statement, since I knew for a fact that Anderson Gallagher had never once been high.

I chuckled at his animation. "A little," I said. His eyes danced at the admission. Before I could wuss out, I reached out and caressed the side of his face. When he didn't immediately pull away, I placed my lips against his. He let out a soft moan as I slipped my tongue past the slight part.

I wasn't sure what I'd been expecting, but it certainly wasn't the distinct response I got. He moved his mouth firmly against mine, deepening the kiss. I'd never believed the ridiculous superstition that red-heads stole souls, but in that moment, it certainly felt like Andy was trying to steal mine.

He really must be high if he's not only letting me kiss him, but kissing me back.

I slid closer, desperately wanting more. Naturally, since he'd said sex was off the table, it was the only thing I could think about.

It's now or never.

I'd thought a lot about what I was about to do. I owed him this at the very least. It wouldn't make up for what I'd done—not by a long shot—but it was a start. More than that, though, I wanted to. And even though I had no idea what I was doing, I wasn't nervous; that's what Andy was for. Andy knew everything.

Our teeth clicked as I deepened the kiss even more to ensure he was properly distracted.

Here goes nothing.

I released his face to slide my hand down his body. Andy was lean in all the right ways and it took an active force of will to stay focused. My hand hit his waistband and immediately slipped into his pants.

He gasped when my fingers wrapped around his erection, effectively breaking the fevered kiss. "Mitch."

I gave a light squeeze, and his eyelids fluttered. He could pretend all he wanted, but his reactions were showing him for the liar he was. He wanted me, even if he refused to admit it.

A firmer squeeze as I dragged up his shaft.

"What are you doing? We talked about this," he said, pushing up to his elbows even as I maneuvered his cock free. Like the rest of him, it was perfect: long, narrow, and stunningly smooth. I gave it another experimental stroke and his breath hitched. "Mitch, I'm serious."

I finally caught his gaze. "I know the rules. Now stop complaining and just tell me how you like it."

"Like wha—?" A strangled moan swallowed the question as I took his shaft in my mouth. I didn't want him to have any reason to deny this, so I took him as deep as I could manage the first time. "Fuck," he hissed.

I took the word as encouragement. I dragged all the way up, pausing at the cap, and did it again. His hand fluttered over my shoulder, then fisted tightly in my hair when I sucked hard on the head. He gave a deeper moan and finally lay back down. I was beyond shocked that he wasn't going to fight me on this. Thrilled at my victory, I pulled him back inside the cavern of my mouth.

"Easy on the teeth," he hissed. I quickly sheathed them with my lips and tried again. His only response this time was to moan. I did it a couple more times, and he added, "Use your hand." I shifted to do as he instructed. "That's it," he sighed as I found a rhythm between my hand and my mouth. "Now swirl your tongue around the tip."

I did and tasted pre-cum. His body shuddered. I added the move to the rest of the formula.

"Just like that," he moaned. "Mmm." His short nails dug into my shoulder. "Yes," he groaned, returning his grip to my hair. As he spoke, his hips rolled up. "Now—"

I didn't let him finish. I took him as deep as I could.

He gave another strangled groan. "Fuck!" Whatever control he'd been exercising vanished. His hips thrust frantically up from the floor as he held my head steady. I let him drive into my mouth, taking what he needed from me, and fought my gag reflex.

He tasted so sweet and I loved that he was clearly enjoying this, but it wasn't enough. I wanted more. I wanted to make him come.

My rhythm returned with renewed vigor as I took back control, adjusting the pattern. Andy moaned deep in his throat as his back arched off the floor. I increased the pressure of my tongue, taking it from base to tip, and swallowed to pull him deeper. He made a high-pitched whine, and I did it again.

"I'm gonna come," he gasped.

Now that I'd found my perfect combo, I wasn't about to relent.

"Seriously. Oh *God*," he groaned. His hand tightened in my hair to the point of pain.

I kept going.

"Mitch—Mitch. You ha-have to stop," he stuttered.

The tip of his cock was practically weeping now. I could taste his imminent orgasm with each stroke. *So close.*

"Stop," he ordered, pulling my hair and forcing me back. His cock made a pop as it came free, and he rolled to the side just in time to ejaculate on the floor.

"Why did you do that?" I asked, not bothering to check my anger.

He didn't answer right away, taking a minute to put himself back together. Finally, he sat up, completely composed, and looked me in the eye. He seemed to choose his words in the face of my obvious irritation. After a moment of studying my expression, he let out a sigh. "Having someone come in you like that is..." He searched for the word. "Different."

I didn't give a shit if it was "different"; that was my choice, and he'd taken it from me. My thoughts must have shown because he gave me a small smile and reached out to hold the side of my face.

"Hey, don't be upset," he said softly. Then he surprised me by leaning forward and placing his lips against mine. The gentle kiss was sweet and tame, lingering. I debated going ahead and deepening it like I wanted to—like I was sure *he* wanted to—then he leaned back. "You're not ready for that yet."

Excitement rushed through me to replace my disappointment—he'd said "yet". The implication alone had me wanting to pull his mouth back.

Before I could, he flopped back, making a noise, and careful to avoid the mess on the floor. "If it's any consolation, that was fucking incredible." He looked delirious as he rolled his head to face me.

I think he might still be a little high.

I tried to focus on the wins I had and resumed my previous position beside him, but stayed propped on my elbow so I could see his expressions better. "Yeah?"

"Yeah," he sighed, turning his gaze back to the ceiling. "I've never walked anyone through it like that," he mused aloud. "You're a quick study." The passive compliment washed over me, lending hope to my crusade. All I'd done was give him head, but the victory felt more substantial.

"I have a good tutor," I responded, settling back down.

He snorted, then yet another laugh attack overtook him. Oh yeah, he was definitely still high. As he sobered back up, he let out a sigh. Tempting this unprecedented easiness between us, I wrapped an arm around his waist. He reflexively turned into it, making the contact more natural.

"What's your favorite part of sex, Andy?" I asked, hoping to keep my streak of wins going.

"Well, the obvious answer is getting off," he replied snidely.

"No shit," I said, jostling him. He laughed like I hoped he would. "Seriously, favorite thing. Before, after, during. Whatever."

"How should I know?" he grumped, sliding closer.

"How should you know? How should you know?" I teased, continuing to jostle him. He released a chorus of laughter. Each new laugh added to the sea of fireflies already filling me.

"Alright. Alright," he said, scooting closer once more, so that if I shook him, I'd shake myself. "Talking afterward is nice."

I scoffed. "Pillow talk is *not* your favorite thing, Andy."

"Oh yeah? What makes you so sure?" he asked over his shoulder.

I tightened my arm around his middle and eliminated the last of the distance between us. For a second, I was transported in time, and it was that night again. Andy felt so innocent curled in the hollow of my body, so right.

Except I'd ruined everything. He wasn't that same innocent boy, but he was still Andy and he was here with me. I nuzzled the back of his neck, inhaling the strange herbal scent he had. "Because I already know what your real favorite thing is," I whispered, giving him a gentle squeeze. A tense minute passed, and I feared I'd just fucked it up all over again.

"How do you know that?" he asked softly. If there had been any other sound in the room, I would never have heard him. Rather than answer, I buried my face in the back of his hair, letting his smell envelop me, and prayed he wouldn't pull away. We both knew how I knew.

Chapter 10

Four Years Ago

Andy

I shivered as I woke, my body aching in both familiar and foreign ways. The night before rushed in to fill me like the best hot cocoa in the world, finding all the tiniest parts of me and suffusing them with warmth. I hummed contentedly and reached out for my best friend. When my hand landed on the cold floor instead, I sat up. I squinted into the dimly lit room as if that would somehow make an extra body magically materialize.

"Mitch?" I whispered, then immediately shook my head. "Way to go, dummy." Another glance around showed his clothes were gone, and obviously he wasn't hiding in one of the nonexistent shadows. There was also no note or any other sign of where he might have gone. I chewed on my bottom lip as I sought my pajamas.

Maybe he didn't leave a note because he's coming right back.

I nearly fell over as I maneuvered my pants on, because damn, that smarted. Truthfully, my body ached more from sleeping on the unforgiving floor than losing my virginity, *that* pain I was more than okay with no matter how difficult it was making getting dressed. One of the giggles I'd fought so valiantly to keep to myself the night before slipped free. I'd never felt so light in my entire life. Yeah, my body hurt like hell, but every sore muscle was absolutely worth it.

"Maybe I don't have to tell him. Maybe he already knows." The hope that had begun as a small ember burned like the sun in my chest. Fear of losing my best friend had made sure I kept my feelings to myself, but now that there was a real chance Mitch might feel the same way about me… Giggles burst free and I immediately clamped a hand over my mouth, my gaze darting to the secret entrance. Which was stupid, really. Hadn't Mitch told me no one could hear us here?

I can't wait to tell him.

I approached the peculiar door and cautiously pushed it away from the wall a crack. In the tiny sliver of the outside world, sunlight filled an arched hallway.

Shit. What time is it?

The door fell back into place as I reassessed the situation. Mitch had probably left already so we wouldn't get caught together and had let me sleep in, because, well, that's just the sort of friend he was.

He's so much smarter than he gives himself credit.

And his heart, fuck, I loved his heart. And his warmth, and his laugh, and now probably his dick. My smile from earlier made a reappearance, and I ventured back to the door.

Now to get from here back to my room without anyone noticing. I smiled wider. *Piece of cake.*

Present Day

Andy

The portrait that hid the secret entrance swung shut and Mitch crowded me against the wall. His hazel eyes flashed in the low lighting and shone with a wildness that instantly had my heart hammering. Strong fingers curled into my hips as our mouths came together like a super magnet. I moaned into him and tangled my fingers in his hair, urging him deeper. He deftly popped my top two buttons and moved to suck a bruise out on my neck. I arched into him and tugged his head back to claim his mouth once more. Mitch didn't argue. He didn't say anything. He never did in my dreams. But knowing it wasn't real didn't change the want coursing through my veins or the need crawling up my spine now, or like it had then. No amount of knowing better could change how badly I wanted him.

His nimble fingers found my fly, and I moaned in anticipation. I knew exactly what it felt like to have Mitch inside of me, owning me like I needed, like only he could, like he always had. Outside, in the real world, I recognized the danger of indulging in the fantasy, but in here, it was safe to want, safe to need. His lips pressed hotly into the side of my neck and I gave over wholly to the sensation. By the time his mouth found mine again, I was panting with desperation and on the verge of begging. The eager kiss gentled, and I sighed into the softness of it. When he pulled back, his eyes held the promise I'd once hung all my hopes and dreams on. I opened my mouth to tell him the truth I should have told him years ago, but before the words could form, something soft smacked forcefully into my head.

My body rocketed back to awareness just in time to catch the next attack. "What the fuck, Lucien?" I snapped as I ripped the pillow away from him. He promptly yanked it back and glared at me.

"You were making gross noises in your sleep. I don't wanna hear that shit." The glower on his face paired well with his tousled, dark hair and sour disposition. I blanched at the implication that my illicit dreams had infringed upon a reality that could and would crucify me.

"Anything else?" I asked, more than a little trite.

He shoved his pillow under his arm and spared me one last menacing glare before stomping back to his bed. While he flopped back down with an irritated huff, I sat up and rubbed at my face. Mercifully, the shock of the rude awakening had done its part to kill my arousal, but sadly, it did nothing for the anxiety now pumping through my veins. More agitated with myself than with Lucien, I flipped the covers back and got dressed. I'd have to be up soon anyway for my meeting with Garza about my application for Chicago's advanced literary program, and this way I could sneak into the breakfast hall early before anyone could find me.

As I slipped out of the room, my mind summoned images better left forgotten. I shoved the memories violently away and hurried to the cafeteria. Unfortunately, the eggs and toast turned to ash in my mouth. I stubbornly drank the entire glass of orange juice so

I could at least pretend I'd acquired sustenance and stalked back out of the slowly filling room. A flash of light filled the hallway, and I altered my course to look out one of the many windows that graced this hall. Rain came down in heavy sheets that obscured the grounds and darkened the sky. A fitting display given my current mood. The day promised to be every bit as dismal as my morning, and I wasn't in the mood for any of it.

My hand tightened on the strap of my satchel as if it could actually ward off the depression clawing at my heart. The dreams weren't new, but they were escalating. Something would need to be done and soon, except I didn't know what. What could I possibly do to alleviate the pain of spending time with Mitch, of indulging in his sudden curiosity? Clearly, allowing him to be blow me had been a mistake of epic proportions and now my reason was off its axis.

I spun away from the window and stalked down the hall, not really sure where I was going until I found myself in the tower. Exhausted, I dropped my bag and slumped to the ground, intending to read until I could face the day. But I didn't take out my latest mystery novel or even the epic fantasy I couldn't seem to finish. Instead, I sat with my back against the wall and watched the rainfall through the large window.

Mitch

I took the stairs two at a time, my heart frantically beating against my ribs. *Please be here.* If he wasn't, I didn't know where else to look. I'd already checked the secret room, his dormitory, and most of the classrooms. I'd even asked people, but no one had seen him beyond Lucien that morning, though he'd looked like he'd swallowed razors at the telling.

Thunder shook the Tower as I launched onto the landing with enough momentum to clear half the small space before coming to a stop. I peered around the room, made darker by the storm raging outside that all but guaranteed no one had ventured beyond the safety of the school. On the verge of despair, a flash of light illuminated the rotunda, and I spotted him against the wall I'd surged past.

"Andy." I breathed a sigh of relief that faltered when he didn't respond. Concern once again took hold as a faint whimper reached my ears. His shadowy form twitched, and the sound came again. I stalked over, but it wasn't until I crouched in front of him I realized he was asleep. "Andy," I tried again with the same result. I reached out, intending to grab his shoulder and shake him awake, but that's not where it ended. I cupped the side of his face and stroked his cheek. "Andy."

"Mitch." He said it so softly, I feared I'd misheard.

I scooted closer until I could feel his deep breathing on my face. "I'm right here." He sighed, and I leaned forward, worried I'd missed another whispered word that could help me understand what was wrong. I was completely unprepared for his lips to brush against mine in a tentative kiss. Taken aback, but unwilling to leave, I softly pressed back. His lips parted with a decidedly different whimper. Then he latched onto me.

He swallowed down my muffled sound of shock and licked inside my mouth. Instinct took over, and I tangled my tongue with his, giving and taking as much as he did. My surprise at the sensual response took a back seat as he continued to kiss me like it was the only thing in the world that mattered. His lips molded to mine like they were made for me and they washed away every thought I had about not fucking this up with the rain falling relentlessly, not ten feet away.

"Andy," I finally managed, my voice ragged with need. The kissing wasn't enough, giving him head wasn't enough. I needed more, needed to make this right.

Suddenly, he jerked back and pressed firmly into the wall. "What the fuck are you doing?" He reached a shadowed hand for his bag. "Seriously, what the hell, Mitch?"

I didn't need to see him to know his eyes were borderline feral or hear his breath coming in short, panicked puffs. My brow furrowed. "What are you talking about? *You* kissed *me*."

"I... I did?" The hint of question only threw me for further of a loop.

"Andy, what's going on?"

"I'm sorry. I... I shouldn't have done that." He scrambled to stand in the narrow space that existed between me and the wall. I rocked back on my heels and rose as he shouldered his bag.

"I don't understand. Is something wrong?" Had I somehow fucked everything up anyway? That would be just my luck, to ruin all of my efforts to get him to forgive me, let me back in, and not even know.

"Why are you here?"

"You skipped all of your classes. That's not like you. I was worried."

"As you can see, I'm fine." He shouldered past me and made for the stairs.

"Andy, wait." He hitched his bag higher and walked faster. "Andy," I called again, but he didn't stop.

Andy

I took the treacherous stairs fast enough to risk falling down them if I mis-stepped, Mitch's voice chasing me the whole way. An entire day of classes missed and for what? To end up having the same nightmare I'd been running away from for four years? Except it hadn't been the same, not really. Unlike the predictable chain of events where I wandered down corridor after corridor, calling for him to come back, begging him to let me try again, this one had been different. This time when I woke in the secret room and called out for him, he'd been there. He'd stepped out of the darkness and held my face tenderly while he laughed about my being a spaz.

I swiped away the sting of tears that remembering the dream brought. He'd kissed my nose and told me he'd never leave me, not ever, that he was here. Then he'd kissed me and every childish dream nurtured in the dark had come true. I kissed him back with everything I had, everything I couldn't put words to, surrendered to the love I so desperately wanted to have. But then he said my name, impossible when his mouth was still firmly glued to mine and I realized the lie for what it was—a dream. Only when I woke up, Mitch was really there, and my lips still tingled from the passionate kiss.

I missed the last step and stumbled to the ground floor. The jarring impact set my teeth on edge, but I pushed on. I needed to get as far away as possible to deal with this wretched fucking day before he could stop me. My frenzied pace slowed, and I sagged against the wall.

What the fuck is wrong with me? I should be past all this.

But clearly, I wasn't if today was anything to go by. I needed to pull it together, and fast. The logical thing to do would be to stop seeing Mitch all together, his curiosity and determination to be friends again be damned. Except I wouldn't and therein lie the problem. I was being tortured all right, but I was the one doing the torturing.

There has to be a way to regain control of this before it spirals anymore out of control. Think.

I rounded the corner and ran into someone hard enough for us both to stumble back. My overstuffed satchel shifted, nearly taking me down with it. I floundered to regain control of my body, as well as my masochistic heart.

"There you are. Where the fuck have you been all day?"

I glanced up from my struggle, surprised to see Calvin. "H-hey."

His eyebrows pulled down, and his mouth pressed into a thin line. "Is everything alright? Where have you been?"

"I..uh…fell asleep in the tower," I forced out as I danced from foot to foot. The V between his eyes deepened.

"What's going on? Who cares if you blew off a few classes? I've blown off plenty."

I shook my head. I'd also missed my meeting with Garza, but that was beside the point. "Mitch found me."

"I'm not surprised," he scoffed. "Especially considering he practically turned this place upside down looking for you."

The comment momentarily distracted me, then I remembered why I couldn't be standing here talking to Calvin. "You don't understand. I was dreaming about…" I glanced behind me to be sure no one was around and leaned closer, "*that* night."

Calvin's eyebrows shot up while his mouth formed an O. "I mean, okay, but so what?"

I leveled a glare at him. "I think I was talking in my sleep. I… I don't know what he may have heard."

"You could always ask him," he suggested, ever the pragmatist.

"No, I can't," I countered without elaborating.

"O-kay, well, you better pull your shit together quick, because he's coming this way." He glanced behind me, lending credence to his words, and I cursed under my breath. "What are you going to do?"

I scrambled for a solution without success. "Cover for me."

"Andy," Calvin said flatly, repositioning his gaze back to me.

"Please."

He bit his lip, then said the last thing I ever expected. "Tell him the truth."

My hackles rose. "No."

"All I'm saying is—"

"I don't give a shit what you're saying," I hissed. "Just be my fucking friend." Shock exploded across his face, but I didn't stick around to see what would come out of his mouth. Mitch had longer legs than me and it wouldn't take him nearly as long to catch up.

I all but raced away, heavy satchel thumping painfully against my leg. There had to be somewhere else I could go, somewhere Mitch wouldn't find me. My usual place was out of the question, though, judging by the torrential rain I could still see falling through the windows. The sound of speedy steps filled the hall, and I glanced back to see if either Calvin or Mitch had followed me. Still looking over my shoulder, I rounded a corner and, for the second time that day, ran into someone.

"Watch where the fuck you're going." At the sound of Benny's voice, my head snapped back forward.

Fuck, like today wasn't bad enough.

I ducked my head and pretended I was invisible as I tried to skirt past him.

"Did you hear me, homo?"

I gritted my teeth and diligently ignored the offensive slur. "Sorry," I said, aiming for meek and growling it instead. His lip curled, and he moved to block my path. "What do you want?" I snapped, beyond exasperated.

"I want you to stop fucking with Mitch." Cold dread slid down my spine. Benny knew. "This is our last season and I don't want this weird ass friendship you two have dicking the team over." My momentary scare dissolved into rage. It was because of people like Benny I'd lost Mitch in the first place.

"Fuck you," I snarled.

"What did you say to me, you ginger freak?" Benny asked, his voice dangerously low as he invaded my space, highlighting the height difference between us.

"You heard me. Fuck. You," I repeated, standing my ground.

His face warped with anger, and his eyes burned with barely contained fury. "You fucking piss-ant, I'm going to—"

I cocked my head to the side, unphased by the looming threat. "Tell me, Benny, had any eventful showers lately?"

"What did you say to me?"

Now it was my turn to get in his face. We all had secrets we'd rather keep in the dark, even Benny. I dropped my voice, but held eye contact so he would know I wasn't kidding. "He still goes to those same showers. Three a.m. like clockwork. Just. In. Case." I let that hang a moment and enjoyed watching the blood drain from his face. "I suggest you take a hard look at yourself before you start passing out names."

Face officially devoid of color, Benjamin Wallace Price IV, school bully extraordinaire, staggered back without a word. I shouldered past him like I had Calvin and continued down the vacant hall. My threat had given me an idea of where to go.

Chapter 11

Mitch

I blew out a breath and flipped the paper over. Nothing about the grade came as a surprise. I'd never excelled at science, and trig-based physics was thoroughly kicking my ass. But not even the deplorable grade could distract from what truly occupied my thoughts and brought me down. I hadn't seen Andy in days, eight to be exact. Sure, we didn't have any classes together, but the school wasn't *that* big. I usually at least saw him around even before we were intentionally spending time together. There wasn't another way to look at it—Andy was avoiding me and had been since whatever had happened in the Tower.

Did I do something wrong?

I wracked my brain, but the only answer forthcoming was that I'd kissed him, or more appropriately, he'd kissed me. *Thoroughly.* Maybe it was because he'd been asleep? He'd certainly seemed awake. How was I supposed to know he hadn't actually woken up when he was—

"You coming?"

I glanced up from my bubble of misery and the hurricane of thoughts clouding it to find Brian's expectant face. Brian was a nice guy, one hell of a defender, and a good friend, but right now there was only one friend on my mind. And he was avoiding me.

I don't understand. We were doing so well, making progress. Or maybe...we weren't? Maybe it's all been in my head and there's really no way Andy will ever forgive me for—

"Did you hear me?" Brian asked as he waved a hand in front of my face. "Where'd you go? You spaced hard there for a minute." Concern tightened his eyes and his mouth turned down. I wasn't stupid. I knew the team was freaking about me being distracted lately, but I also knew I'd stay distracted until I figured this thing with Andy out.

As I stood, I slung my bag over my shoulder, then grabbed the test. "Sorry, man. A lot on my mind. Right now, though, I need to talk with Cohen about some extra credit." Brian winced. Extra credit from Cohen wasn't something anyone ever wanted to need. Lessons were bad enough. They were worse when you had to endure them twice, and that was assuming he was willing to offer any credit in the first place.

"That bad?"

"That bad," I echoed. He gave me a sympathetic shake of his head, then left me to my groveling.

Cohen glanced up as I approached his desk, not an ounce of surprise on his lightly tan face. "Mr. Hudson."

"Hey Mr. C, about my grade—"

"You know I don't subscribe to Coach Santinelli's assertion that anyone on the team gets a pass. There are no handouts here."

"I know," I mumbled, absolutely mortified. "That's not what I want."

Surprise finally registered on his face as raised eyebrows, though the rest of his expression remained unsettlingly neutral. "What did you have in mind?"

"I was hoping you could assign me some real extra credit?"

His features softened with sympathy, and he leaned forward to rest his forearms on the desk. "I don't mean to be cruel, Mitch, but all the extra credit in the world won't help if you don't understand the material."

"Yeah," I sighed, looking down at my feet and scooting a rogue button with my shoe. *Fuck, even the teacher thinks I'm hopeless.*

"Gallagher was tutoring you, was he not? Have you considered asking him for help on this subject as well?"

My heart landed with an unpleasant squelch in my stomach. Oh, I'd thought about it alright, along with about a million other things I was positive would never happen. "I think he might be done helping me."

Professor Cohen considered me a long minute, then leaned back and pulled open a drawer. He took out a thick packet and held it out. "He'll help, I'll make sure of it. You two can start with this workbook. It covers all the material that was on the last exam and some of what will be on the next."

My fingers wrapped around the unexpected offering.

"Anderson is familiar with the material, and it shouldn't take him long to get into it. Complete that entire book, showing your work," he gestured to the test clutched in my other hand, "and we'll see about raising that a letter grade or two. It should also give you a good foundation for the midterm. Ace that, and you'll be well on your way to graduating with a B minus."

I pulled the book closer, stuck between happy shock and crushing disbelief. All of this was pointless if Andy wouldn't be in the same room as me. "How are you going to get him to help?"

"I have my ways." Cohen winked, then pulled out his phone, tapped out a quick message, and returned it to the drawer.

"Uh…" I trailed off, suddenly anxious that my desire to pass the damn subject had inadvertently gotten Andy into trouble. That certainly wouldn't help my case.

"Don't worry, nothing untoward. Promise. A little birdie told me Anderson is hoping Garza will write him a recommendation letter for his application to Chicago U's advanced program. Rest assured, Garza will ensure that he's enthusiastic about the assistance."

"Oh. You sure?" I asked, still not convinced that Andy wouldn't resent me for jeopardizing his chances.

"Positive. I'm also pleased to see you finally taking a genuine interest in your grades. Any particular reason?"

"I don't want to take an athletic scholarship," I whispered, knowing full well that if word got back to coach, he'd have a stroke. Cohen's eyebrows rose once more and his mouth fell open. I didn't blame him. As far as he knew, as far as everyone knew, I lived, slept, and breathed lacrosse. Everyone but Andy. He recovered from his shock, snapping his mouth shut, and busied himself reorganizing his already pristine desk.

"In that case, we'll have to see what we can do about that grade. Won't we?"

Andy

I stomped down the abandoned hallway, still bristling from the meeting with my mentor. I couldn't believe Garza was holding my letter of recommendation hostage in order to get me to tutor someone. And not even in literature. Ridiculous didn't cover it. Ludicrous was more like it. Or maybe even outrageous. But without that letter, I'd never get into the advanced writing program. Still grumbling to myself and mentally running through a thesaurus of vitriol, I pushed open the door to professor Cohen's classroom and stopped dead.

The hopeful smile melted off of Mitch's face and I could only imagine what my own looked like. "They didn't tell you," he said. Not a question, a statement of fact. He shook his head and averted his gaze. After a few moments of tense silence in which I remained frozen in the door, he scooped his books off the table into his bag. "It's okay. I'll… I'll figure something else out."

My heart sank at seeing his obvious disappointment and hearing the hint of despair that colored his words. Was I really going to punish him—punish his grades—because I couldn't keep the past and present separate? When he'd needed a friend the most, he'd turned to me. That had to count for something, right? He stood, and I stepped deeper into the room, letting the door swing silently shut behind me.

"Wait."

"It's fine, Andy. I… understand if you don't want to be around me."

My heart twisted painfully. That wasn't the case at all, it would never be the case. Of course I wanted to be around him—I'd be glued to him if I could. And that right there was the root of the problem. Even after everything that had happened over the last four years, I still wanted to be his best friend.

"That's not—" My voice cracked, and I regathered myself. After a deep breath, I pushed through the fear that I wouldn't survive this. "That's not true. I'll help." I walked into the room beneath his wary gaze and took a seat in the chair beside where he remained standing. "Garza said you'd have a workbook. Can I see it?" He didn't so much as twitch or blink. "Please," I added.

He stared down at me, uncertainty darkening his hazel eyes. "You don't have to do this. I'll tell Cohen I changed my mind and not to let Garza take it out on you."

"I know I don't have to. I want to," I said without an iota of hesitation.

"Really?" He sank back into his seat, disbelief still evident on his face.

"Really. Now, how about that workbook?" I smiled softly in the hope it would lend credence to my assertion. Because, damn it all, I did want to help, and I *hated* physics, which Garza damn well knew.

Mitch blinked and twisted to retrieve the requested item from his bag. "Did you wanna see the test? I won't lie, it's pretty bad."

"No."

His head whipped around, the hand holding the promised workbook following much slower with the rest of his torso. "Why not?"

I shrugged. "Because it doesn't matter."

"But—"

"But nothing." I placed a hand over his where it had settled on the table still clutching the thick packet like it was a life raft. "It's in the past and we're going to change it." I winked at him and tugged the workbook free of his grasp so I could flip through and scan the pages. "Plus, it sounds like you've beat yourself up about it plenty. All that's left is to move forward and do better now, wouldn't you say?" I glanced over at him, because he'd yet to utter a syllable.

"Do you really believe that?" The question came out thick, laced with an emotion that I couldn't quite put my finger on and that, admittedly, surprised me.

"If I didn't, I wouldn't be here." Forget the fact that Garza had blackmailed me here under false pretenses. The second I realized it was Mitch, I could have left. I'd figure my shit out and find a way to make this work, enjoy whatever weird game Mitch was playing, because at the end of the day, any time I could steal with him would be worth the inevitable heartache. I cleared my throat and let out a laugh that I prayed he wouldn't recognize as nervous. "Please tell me you brought a calculator."

His lips quirked up in a hesitant smile that grew with confidence until it popped a dimple in his cheek. "Nope."

Chapter 12

Andy

I rubbed my hands down my face as I tried to convince myself for probably the thousandth time that I could do this. But this wasn't editing a paper and giving it back. This would be shoulder to shoulder, constant proximity studying. With Mitch. And I was already doing a shit-tastic job of keeping my emotions in check. I dropped my head back to stare at the ceiling of my dorm room and let out a groan.

"What's got you so blue?" Lucien asked as he stepped into the room with a few books tucked under his arm. At first glance, they all seemed to be textbooks, but further inspection revealed a worn paperback tucked between the school books.

I straightened up and rolled my shoulders to loosen the tension build up. Unsurprisingly, it had zero success.

Lucien set his books down and considered me for a moment. "You had your meeting with your mentor the other day, right? Did it not go well?"

"It certainly could have gone better," I grumbled, stalking over to my bed and sitting with a huff.

My roommate's eyebrows lifted. "Really? I thought everything was on track for your application to Chicago."

I waved a dismissive hand. "It's not the application, per se."

"Then what?" Lucien swiveled his desk chair around and plopped into it, propping his elbows on his knees as he leaned forward.

"Garza is *encouraging* me to tutor another student. Insists that it will look good on my application." Why I didn't come right out and tell him who I was tutoring was beyond me. Probably because I was having a difficult time wrapping *my* head around agreeing in the first place.

Lucien leaned back and frowned. "Is it one of the younger kids? I get how that can be a pain, but surely it won't be all that bad. Not that I think you need *anything* else padding your application," he added with a smirk.

I almost returned it, but the reality of the truth kept my lips in a firm line. "I wish. No, it's another senior in our year. But get this, it's not even in literature."

He held up a hand and shook his head. "Okay, you've officially lost me. What the hell does Garza have you tutoring if it's *not* literature?"

"Physics," I deadpanned and watched Lucien's expression go from mild curiosity to full-blown confusion.

"What the hell?"

"Oh, it gets better. I'm tutoring Mitch." Maybe if I shared, had someone to help keep me accountable, remind me in a round-about way that *wanting* to be around Mitch was not a good thing, I'd actually survive this somehow. Also, wouldn't hurt to have the explanation for why we'd suddenly be spending so much time together.

Lucien barked a laugh, but when I didn't join him, he speared me with a disbelieving stare. "Wait. You're serious? Like Mitch—Mitch Hudson—Mitch? The school's star lacrosse player and grade-A asshat. That Mitch?"

Well, now I knew exactly how Lucien felt about my would-be pupil. "The one and only."

"Okay, maybe it's not *all* bad. You two used to be good friends, right?"

I leaned back on my elbows and hoped Lucien hadn't seen the flash of pain that statement always brought me. "Emphasis on the 'used to'."

"Shit, man, that sucks. Couldn't you tell Garza no? I mean, sure, it could look good on your app, but it's not Lit and you don't really need it."

"I do, however, need Garza's letter of recommendation if I want to secure a spot in the advanced writing program, which he's currently holding hostage. Without his Alumnus endorsement, I might as well not even bother applying to Chicago." Maybe should have checked my bitterness... While I didn't agree with what Garza was doing, it wasn't really him I was mad at, or Mitch, for that matter. I was mad at myself, because apparently getting ghosted and ignored for four years wasn't enough for me to get over my first crush...first love.

"That's fucked."

I pointed at Lucien. "You said it." I shifted back to a properly seated position and indicated the worn paperback on his desk. "Now you going to tell me about what you're reading or what?" I asked, seeking more familiar territory for us. Lucien and I got along fairly well for two guys that had randomly been assigned as room-mates—we both despised sports, were top of our classes, and we loved to read. What we didn't do was make a habit of talking heavy shit. Sure, we'd covered our fair share of family drama, but it was few and far between. And while Lucien might not know it, Mitch was heavy shit. So books.

"Dude," Lucien said with a wide grin as he reached for the book. "This thing has got dragons, like all kinds, and witches, and fae, and what have you." He leaned forward again, checked the door, and despite it being closed, dropped his voice. "It also has sex. Like *a lot* of sex." His eyes widened comically, and I couldn't help but chuckle.

"And who gave you this hella racy book?"

Lucien shrugged. "It's on loan from my sister."

"Your sister?" I echoed. "Isn't that a little…weird?"

"Maybe, but when I saw her a couple of weeks back, she accused me of always reading the same things. Said I needed to 'broaden my horizons' and threw it at me. I told her I could read anything she did, and here we are."

I chuckled again. "Sibling rivalry gets you every time." And wouldn't I know it, being the youngest—and shortest—of three.

"No shit," Lucien said with a huff.

"But you *like* dragons? And I doubt you've never read a book without some kind of sex in it. How is this any different?"

Lucien's face went from its usual tawny chestnut to full on burnt red. He cleared his throat, then before continuing in the same low whisper as before, checked the closed door…again. "It's not *just* a lot of sex, it's a lot of different *kinds* of sex."

Now it was my turn to be shocked. I couldn't help but follow the book as Lucien flipped it around in his hands. Was it possible the book had gay dragon sex? I'd never read a book with gay sex at all. They weren't exactly plentiful at the bookstore in town and I couldn't buy them when I was home for breaks, as my family had no clue I was gay. What I really wanted to do was ask Lucien if I could read it next. But that would be weird, right? Then again, we shared books all the time. Surely this wouldn't be any different just because he'd admitted to it having adventurous sex.

I was about to go for it when Lucien cleared his throat again and ducked his head. He shoved the book into his side table drawer so fast he probably bent the cover. "Anyway, the—story is solid and no way am I gonna let Amari get one up on me for this. She'll now if I chickened out and DNF-ed."

"Can't have that," I said, more than a little disappointed that he hadn't even offered.

"Also, she...um, wants it back the next time I visit." Lucien looked abashed, his cheeks still pink from his confession. "So I'm kind of on a time limit, what with fall break coming up. Sorry." He gave me a weak smile.

Technically, fall break was still *several* weeks away and more than enough time for both of us to read the book, but Lucien had made his position clear. He wasn't comfortable sharing something like that, which was a real bummer, because now curiosity was clawing away inside of me.

Wonder if I could sneak a few peeks at it without him knowing.

"So Mitch..."

I blinked and dragged my attention away from the denied book. "What about him?" I asked dubiously.

"He really as good a player as everyone says?"

"Wouldn't know. Never been to a single match and don't know a damn thing about the game."

Lucien grimaced. "Sounds like your tutoring lessons are going to be a special kind of torture."

I let out a heavy sigh, picturing Mitch's shirt plastered to his toned body. I may not have been to any games, but thanks to Calvin, I'd seen my fair share of practices. "You have no idea."

"You know what? We're both done with classes for the day. Let's go into town and hang out for a bit. What do you think?" Lucien waited patiently for my answer.

Finally, I nodded. "Yeah, that would…that would be nice." I pushed off the bed and we both switched out of our uniforms for casual wear, then set off for town. Luckily, the weather had cooled, and it wasn't oppressively hot as we made the twenty-minute trek into town. We even lucked out with a pleasant breeze. By the time we'd sauntered onto Main Street in Hylestead, I'd all but forgotten about the stressful situation with Mitch, but not so much about the racy paperback still sequestered in Lucien's side table.

He pointed at the bookstore. "Wanna go in?"

"Since when do we *not*?" I snorted and opened the door so he could go in first. We both waved to the clerk on duty, then gravitated toward the shelves, Lucien toward the fantasy section and me toward the murder mysteries. After about half an hour of independent perusing, we regrouped.

"What did you find?" Lucien asked as he rearranged his own stack of finds.

I pulled out a used copy of *Murder, She Wrote*. "Thought it might be fun to check out some classics."

He shook his head and laughed. "You know, if I didn't know you so well, I'd be worried."

"What's that supposed to mean?" I asked, clutching the book and several others in the series to my chest.

"It's just murder, murder, murder all the time with you."

I scowled at him. "Is not."

Lucien's dark eyebrows lifted. "Oh yeah? When's the last time you read something that *wasn't* about people getting axed?"

"They don't all get axed… Sometimes they get shot, or poisoned, or runover. But that's beside the point. I read other things."

He put down the rest of his stack and crossed his arms. "Yeah. Like what?"

"You're not the only one who occasionally dips their toe into romance," I replied with a smirk, unable to resist the dig.

His face fell into a hard scowl. "Okay, smartass. Try this one out." He plucked a book free of a nearby shelf. "It's the first book in a duology. It's got magic, mayhem, and, yes, plenty of death for your morbid soul."

I took the proffered book and wrinkled my nose, not exactly enthusiastic about reading a book about daughters, first or otherwise.

"Don't let the title fool you. It's a great story." Lucien levelled a look at me as he picked up his collection. "At least give it a shot. If you decide you hate it, I'll buy it from you."

"Deal." We made our way to the checkout, laughing as we purchased the latest design of the store's canvas bag to hold our acquisitions, then ventured back into the town.

Lucien smacked me in the arm, nearly throwing me and the bag. "Let's hit up that pizza place."

"Ugh, yes! My kingdom for a slice of pepperoni."

"You're such a dork," he said with a laugh that I echoed.

"And you're not?"

"Pft. Not as much as *you*," he fired back as we turned onto the street with the pizza place.

I lurched to a stop, and laughter stuck in my throat. Leaving the pizza parlor was a rowdy group of guys, laughing and cutting up. And at their heart was Mitch. His radiant smile simultaneously lifted my heart and ruthlessly stabbed it. Would he ever laugh like that with me again?

Lucien stopped a pace later and glanced between me and the group. "Andy?"

I struggled to respond, but couldn't tear my gaze from Mitch as the entire group continued to approach. I'd always been so careful never to run into him in town, confident that my reaction would give me away…kind of like it was now. The group got right up beside us and I held my breath.

Mitch turned his smile on me. And while it was probably a trick of the imagination, it seemed to become even brighter. "Hey, Andy. See you Thursday?"

I tried unsuccessfully to swallow and nodded. "Yeah. Thursday."

Mitch's eyes crinkled with his grin, and my stupid heart skipped a beat. Then he turned to one of his companions and they kept going. I couldn't help but stare after them while I fought with my longing to be the one beside him instead of the one left behind.

"Maybe studying with Mitch won't be so torturous after all," Lucien said, snapping me out of my stupor.

I gave myself a good internal shake and moved to catch up to him. "Oh trust me, it'll be torture."

Chapter 13

Mitch

The book made an ominous thud as Andy dropped it to the table. His laugh at my expression almost wiped away my doubt that I'd ever grasp this material. We'd already had a handful of tutoring sessions, much to the dismay of my teammates, as they regularly coincided with informal practices.

"Don't look so discouraged," Andy said, smacking my arm and returning his attention to the heavy text. "I promise, this will make it easier."

"For you maybe. You're a freaking genius."

"Aw, thanks." Despite the teasing response, he noticeably brightened at the praise.

"I'm serious, Andy. I can't even grasp trigonometry. How am I supposed to understand calculus?"

"And I'm serious, *Mitch*. This will help. They're two different types of math. Trust me when I say I think you'll have an easier go with calculus."

I grumbled to myself, then leaned back, tilting my chair on its back two legs, and crossed my arms. "You could just tell me there's no hope instead of trying to teach me a whole other subject in four weeks."

He let out a huff that sounded like a volume of frustration, then turned to me. "You're a stubborn ass. Quit with the doom and gloom or I'm making you write lines."

The threat provoked a snicker out of me. "Pretty sure you don't have that authority."

He raised a red brow, his green eyes sparking a challenge. "Try me."

I leaned forward, sending the chair crashing back to the Earth. Our faces hovered inches apart as we stared each other down in silence. His green eyes bored into mine without mercy or a single blink, perfectly resolute and convinced of his ultimate victory.

Bet if I captured his mouth and pinned him onto the table, he'd blink.

The rogue thought popped up out of nowhere, nearly disrupting my own efforts not to blink. I pushed it away, refusing to entertain letting the mindless need that lived inside of me anywhere near Andy…again. He shifted, but still didn't bat an eye. Something red popped up in my periphery and I did a double take.

"Ha!" Andy crowed in victory. "I win. Calculus it is and you don't get to bellyache about it."

I blinked again and reached for the object of my distraction—a cup of chocolate pudding.

He snatched it away before my fingers could close around it, and I shifted my shock to him. His eyes glinted with mischief and barely contained mirth. "You can have it… *After* you hear me out."

"Are you…bribing me?" My gaze shifted to the hostage snack. "With pudding?"

"You accomplish more with the carrot than the stick."

I barked out a laugh, then doubled over as they kept coming. "And you say *I* use outdated phrases. What did you do, look that up?"

He shifted in his seat and set the pudding on his other side. Not far enough that I couldn't reach it, though. All it would take was getting practically on top of him to snag it with my longer arms. Which I wouldn't do, because then I'd be pressed against him and there was no telling what I would do.

A smile tweaked the corners of his mouth as he focused on the text. "Maybe," he admitted.

I stopped thinking about what it would take to get the pudding and how I was likely to forget all about the treat if I got that close to him and gave Andy my undivided attention. "Let's hear it. How the hell is calculus going to help?"

"Did you know calculus was invented to explain physics?"

"You can invent math?"

He laughed and scooted closer, bringing the book along with him. The smell of his herbal soap drifted beneath my nose. I breathed out heavily to clear it so I could think straight. "I want you to look at this." He pointed to a section of the page with a picture of light being refracted through a bubble into a miniature rainbow.

"Pretty."

He glanced up at me, his mouth twisted into a frown. "Does any of this look familiar?"

I dragged my attention away from the shapes his mouth was making to read the page. It took three passes, all of which Andy sat perfectly quiet through, until it clicked. Without a word, I yanked out the physics text that rivaled his calculus book and plopped it on the table. A few flips later, I landed on a page with an almost identical image.

"What the fuck?" I glanced back and forth between the long, complicated formula on my page and the short, straightforward one on his. "What the fuck?" I said again.

He laughed and slid over the pudding along with a magically produced spoon. "Willing to listen now?"

I snatched the snack, peeled back the lid, and shoved a spoonful in my mouth. Beside me, Andy watched me with an unreadable expression. I took a slightly less aggressive bite and looked over at him. "Did you want some?"

He shook his head quietly, then seemed to register he was staring. He shook himself and pointed back to the similar pages. "The bad news is that you still have to learn the trig way." I nearly choked on my latest spoonful. He glanced at me out of the corner of his eye, then continued, "But the good news is that you can use this to check your work."

"I don't see how that helps my current problem, seeing as how trig *is* the problem."

"It's not perfect, but I think if you knew you were on the right track, what the reward would be," he pointed at the now empty cup in my hand, "then you wouldn't be so quick to believe you can't do it." His fierce gaze softened. "You're smarter than you give yourself credit for, always have been."

In that moment, I wanted more than anything to kiss Andy, to grab his face and own his mouth, to thank him for believing in me, for being my friend, for giving me a second chance. I pushed past the overwhelming desire, not the least of which because the last time I'd gotten too excited and done just that, he'd freaked. "Okay," I said, discarding the empty cup and scooting my chair closer so that we were huddled together over the texts, "how do we do this?"

Andy

I paced the small room for what was likely the thousandth time, filled with just as much anxious energy as I usually had before I'd pull off a prank. Except this was so much more than a prank. This was Mitch's future. He needed to blow that midterm out of the water if he had any hope of redeeming his grade for this class, not to mention his overall GPA. Of course, if he took an athletic scholarship, no one would care what his grades were as long as he hadn't outright failed.

But if I'd deduced nothing over the last five weeks, it was that Mitch didn't want to be defined by a sport anymore. That, and I had zero sense of self preservation. Hours spent shoulder to shoulder, thigh to thigh, had only fueled more dreams that wouldn't be ignored. Admitting to myself that I enjoyed spending time with Mitch was a hell of a lot harder than it should have been. But I couldn't help it. Every minute we spent together seemed to bring him closer to *my* Mitch, the Mitch I'd lost all those years ago.

A swath of afternoon light cut across the floor and I looked up right as the secret door swung shut. "Took you fucking long enough."

"You try sneaking in here in the middle of last bell," he fired back.

Right, last bell, I'd nearly forgotten. I'd been so eager to learn the results that I'd begged off my last class of the day and headed straight here. Rather than admit how anxious I was, I waved a dismissive hand. "Do you have the results or not?"

He gave me a crooked smile and flashed that damned dimple as he pulled out a manila envelope, sealed just like the one Garza had given him. I surged forward, already reaching for it, only to be stopped by Mitch's hand on my chest. "Curse you and your long arms," I grumbled as I pushed against the immovable barrier, my fingers curling in the air well short of their goal.

"Someone's impatient," he laughed while continuing to hold me at bay.

I let out a huff and dropped my arms. "You're not the only one who worked hard for that."

"Suppose you have a point." He let his hand fall and walked to the center of the small space. There, he lowered his school bag to the ground, where it slumped over on its side while he fingered the seal. I joined him and took a steadying breath that did absolutely nothing to quell my tide of nerves.

Please don't let me have failed him.

"Here." He shoved the envelope in my hands.

"What?"

"You open it."

I made to pass it back. "Mitch, I can't..."

He pushed it back toward me. "Please?"

I took a moment to register his own state of nerves—the pinched line of his mouth, the wariness in his eyes, the tightness pulling his shoulders together—and nodded. I used my thumb to peel back the tacky flap, then glanced at him again before pulling out the results. To my surprise, Cohen hadn't given him the usual single-page report. He'd given him the entire hefty exam.

Probably so we can review any errors.

"Well? How bad is it? I know you don't sugarcoat, but maybe make an exception this time?" Mitch licked his lips, and I followed his gaze back to the pages in my hand and the circled grade. At seeing the red number, my chest swelled with pride and it took every ounce of willpower not to crow with delight.

"No need."

"Fuck." He dropped his head back and squeezed his fists against his eyes. "I knew it was too much to hope for. So much for thinking I did well."

Some of my excitement bubbled over and I laughed. "No, Mitch, there's no need to sugarcoat, because you did fine, better than fine. You aced it."

He straightened and snatched the exam from me. "I did?"

"You totally did." Pride radiated from my chest to glow in each nerve ending.

Mitch glanced back up at me with my grin threatening to split my face in two. "Is that… That says ninety-eight. Does that say ninety-eight?"

"Yeah, yeah it does."

He ran a hand through his hair and stared down at the page in disbelief mixed with wonder. "Holy fuck. We did it."

"*You* did it," I corrected. The pride coursing through my veins turned to raw energy that had me vibrating in place. Taking a page out of his playbook, I surged forward and slammed him with a bruising kiss. Unlike when he'd done it to me, he only had a moment of shock before responding in kind.

The exam fell heavily to the floor as he opened up and kissed me back just as hard. The energy inside me turned white hot and blindingly bright. Nice as the kiss was, it wasn't enough. I needed more of an outlet before I was burned from the inside out. I continued to snatch at his lips while my fingers found his buckle. Once it was free, I tackled the button. Mitch pulled back with a gasp and released his hold on my head, though fuck if I knew when it had gotten there.

"Andy, what are you doing?" he asked as I slipped a hand past his waistband.

I hummed with delight at finding him already hard and stole another kiss before falling to my knees. "Should think it's pretty obvious." I tugged his briefs down to reveal my prize. His erection bounced free, the head already swollen red, and my mouth watered.

"You don't have to do this."

I grabbed hold of him and heat pulsed through my hand to fill the rest of me. "Would have thought you'd caught on by now that I don't do anything I don't want to." I brushed my thumb over his slit and leaned forward.

"Andy." I glanced up at the insistence in his voice. His chest heaved with rapid breaths and the flush of arousal stained his cheeks while his fingers dug sharply into my shoulder to keep me at bay.

"Trust me," I said softly, and bypassed my original destination to place a gentle kiss on the side of his cock. He shuddered and the hand gripping my shoulder relaxed ever so slightly. I lay a trail of delicate kisses down his shaft until I could bury my nose in his groin. The intense musk of him swallowed me whole, and I barely suppressed a groan of need. Mitch had no such reservations, as his own groan sounded like it was ripped from a strangled throat.

I rocked back on my heels and licked my lips in anticipation. This time, when I leaned forward, he didn't stop me. I took my time pulling him in, savoring the feel of velvet over steel. When his length edged the back of my throat, I hummed in contentment. Why the hell had I waited so long to taste him? I took him a fraction deeper before wrapping my tongue around him and working my way back to the tip. His haggard moan was the perfect encouragement. I seriously doubted this was the first time Mitch Hudson had ever gotten head, but I'd be damned if it wouldn't be the best.

Mitch

I threaded my fingers through Andy's thick, red hair, shining copper in the light, and focused on not letting my knees buckle. Fuck, was this really happening? My mind couldn't wrap around it at all. One minute I'd been staring at the highest grade I've ever gotten in science, the next, Andy was on his knees with my dick in his mouth.

The barest hint of teeth brushed over my increasingly sensitive dick. I hissed and tightened my hold on his hair. I felt as much as heard him snicker as he swallowed around me. Fuck, that felt good. My grip relaxed as he found a steady rhythm, his tongue routinely wrapping around my shaft like he'd found the best damn lollipop in the world. I slid my fingers through his hair and refused to give into the urge to ram down his throat until I came or collapsed.

He pulled back with a slurping pop. I looked down as he continued to stroke me, but he wasn't looking at me. Without warning, he lapped at my sac, then promptly sucked a ball into the heat of his mouth.

"Mother of God!" I cried out. My relaxed hold on his hair turned white-knuckle as I rode out the sensation. He released it only to lavish attention on the other and my hold on him became the only thing keeping me upright. Fuck, why hadn't I thought to do this for him? No sooner did I adjust to the latest tide of stimulation than he swallowed my dick back down. I let out a strangled moan that he echoed. "Shit, sorry," I said and forced my hand to stop pulling sharply on his hair.

He hummed like he had earlier, and the vibrations rippled through my cock to wrap around the base of my spine. Fuck, I wasn't going to last much longer. Already my fingers tingled with the promise of imminent release. *Warn…need to warn him.* The thoughts came sluggishly as they forced themselves through the haze of mind-blowing sensation.

"A-Andy." His name came out raw and barely audible. I swallowed the zero moisture in my mouth. "And-dy, I'm… I'm gonna…" He swallowed me deeper than he had before and I lost the words. I lost everything as I shot down his throat. My fingers tightened in his hair once more and he moaned, but there wasn't a damn thing I could do about loosening the hold as my orgasm tore through me like a freight train. He finished licking me clean and I finally relinquished my death grip on his hair only to fist a hand in his shirt and drag him to his feet.

"Mi—"

I slammed my mouth on his, not caring that I could taste myself on his tongue. In fact, I sought out every trace of seed I could find until all that was left was Andy, pure, perfect Andy. At last, I pulled away, solely by virtue of the fact that I was out of breath. "Holy fucking shit, Andy. That was…" *Unexpected. Incredible. Insane.*

"An A-plus." He smirked, obviously satisfied with reducing me to an incoherent mess that couldn't finish a sentence.

"Fuck you." I laughed and yanked him in close, wrapping my arms around him, pinning his own between us, and rested my head on his. "Fuck," I repeated as I panted in his hair. By some miracle I hadn't actually pulled any of it out, though not for lack of trying. When my breathing finally got back under control, I whispered, "You didn't have to do that."

"I know," he said into my chest.

I counted it a special kind of victory that he hadn't pulled away yet and tightened my hold around him. While my body relaxed, my mind whirled in a million directions, most of which centered around how incredible the last ten minutes of my life had been.

Damn, Andy is good at that. Like really, really good.

I wasn't so naïve to think it would be the best blowjob I'd ever have, but it certainly held the record to date. My sigh of utter relaxation was halfway out when the realization of how Andy would have gotten so good at giving head finally sank in. The breath lodged in my throat and I lurched back. Andy on his knees for a bunch of faceless guys was not something I wanted to envision, but too late. The damage was done.

Andy tilted his head to the side and frowned as I put myself away, then leaned down to snatch the test off the floor. He followed my jerky movements, the concern on his face deepening. "Mitch?" I moved to grab my bag, and he placed a hand on my arm, halting me in my tracks. "Are you okay? Are...*we* okay?"

The uncertainty in his voice made me want to die. "Yeah," I croaked, not even the least bit believably.

"What is it?"

I grabbed at the first thing that came to mind. "You swallowed."

His eyes widened with surprise. "I knew what I was doing."

The image of Andy kneeling for some faceless stranger flashed again. I forced the image back with a rage that unnerved me, then proceeded to pummel the ever-loving shit out of it.

Something must have shown on my face, because he immediately added, "Shit. I didn't mean to upset you." The unexpected worry snapped me out of my downward spiral.

"What? No. I'm not…upset." A lie, but not the one he'd think. "I feel…" I floundered once more for something to fill the blank, anything to explain my weird ass reaction to getting blown by my best friend, literally the best of my life thus far. "Guilty." The word left my lips and dropped like a stone that grew until it filled the entire room.

Why the fuck did I say that?

Andy grabbed my bag from the ground while I remained frozen and incapable of breathing. A small smile turned up the corners of his mouth as he draped the strap over me, then placed his hands on my chest. Warmth pooled where his fingertips rested. I couldn't help but wonder if he could feel my heart racing beneath his palm or could tell that my lungs seemed to have forgotten how to work.

"You have nothing to feel guilty about." He rose on his toes and brushed his lips lightly over mine before lowering back down. "I'm really proud of you, Mitch." I stared into his green eyes framed with copper and took a shaky breath. He blinked as I let it out slowly and drew another. His freckles bunched as his smile grew. "What do you say we go acquire ourselves some well-earned pudding from the kitchen?"

"That sounds like a good idea."

"I agree," he said as he took the test from my limp fingers, slipped it back into the forgotten envelope, then secured it safely back in my bag. He turned away to grab his own things, then led the way to the secret door. He peered out into the hall, glanced over his shoulder at me, and eased out of the opening. I followed mutely after him, knowing now what I'd known all those years ago—Anderson Gallagher had the power to destroy me. The question was, would he still be there to pick up the pieces when he did?

Chapter 14

Mitch

Every muscle burned as I made a break for the goal. Dalton, our primary goalie, took a defensive stance in the crease, prepared to stop the play Brian and I were running. Brian skid short of the crease, but when the ball left his net, it didn't hurtle into the goal.

I swiveled on my heel, sweat streaming down my bare back, to catch the rubber ball flying toward me. As I turned, a flash of copper on the hillside snagged my attention. Andy. I did a double take. And Calvin. For a split second, I forgot about the ball racing toward me and fully capable of giving me a concussion. Was Andy here for me? Or was he here because Calvin was here? Calvin almost always watched our practices. The entire team knew; it wasn't like he was sly about it. But it was also an unspoken agreement, similar to the one I'd made about Andy, that Calvin was Benny's problem. If Benny wasn't doing anything about it, then none of us were going to bother either.

"Hudson!" Santinelli shouted from the sideline.

I shook off the distraction and held up my stick in time to get body-checked. Blue sky filled my vision as I hit the ground hard enough to crack my back and knock all the air from my lungs. I blinked in a daze as clouds lazily drifted across the sky far above and transported me back to a different time.

Andy and I were laying in the grass on a hot summer day. He'd come to visit me for a couple weeks and I'd just told him about how my father had died before I'd come to UPA. Unsurprisingly, he'd been supportive and empathetic, asking me questions about my dad, but never pushing. He even understood that I was still kind of angry at him.

At one point, while we were calling out shapes in the clouds, we'd gone into a companionable silence. Then he'd said that while he wasn't really religious, he believed my dad was still out there. Stating that energy could neither be created nor destroyed and at their core, wasn't that what souls were anyway? Pure energy. So, really, how cool was it that my dad was out there? He could be anything. A star, part of a new planet, maybe even a comet or black hole. But wherever he was, he was part of the fabric of the universe—just like I was.

He'd looked at me with those bright green eyes of his, a soft smile curling his lips. I knew then what I'd known the first time I'd met him, I—

"Mitch? Mitch. Can you hear me?"

I blinked a few times, but instead of Andy's warm eyes, Nate's dark blue ones greeted me. The happy memory continued to slip away like mist dissipating with the dawn. I groaned and rolled to my side.

"Shit, man. That was brutal. You alright?" Nate took a step back as I sat up and braced my stick across my knees, my breathing still pretty labored.

"Yeah. I'll be good."

"Hudson!" Coach shouted again as he stalked closer. "This is no time for chasing butterflies. Get your head in the game. You're no good to me if you're not on your feet." He jerked his thumb violently toward the locker rooms. "Hit the showers. Hawthorne, you go with him. Next time I see you out here, Hudson, your head better not be up your ass." With that, Santinelli stormed off, already barking orders at the rest of the team to get their shit together.

I fought the urge to hurl my stick at Santinelli's fat head. Fucking asshole.

"Come on, we better get going before he comes back." Nate extended a hand that I gratefully took. Without his help, I probably would have fallen back on my ass. "You good?" he asked again as he helped steady me.

I took a deep breath that felt like fire in my lungs and let it out slowly. "I'll live." We trudged in silence toward the lockers and I glanced over at him, noting the pinched line between his brows and the way his lips were pressed into a thin line. "I'm sorry."

"What for? It's not like you asked John to freaking demolish you."

I shook my head, though I couldn't say I was surprised. Despite hanging with the same crowd for years, I wasn't entirely convinced John actually liked me. "It's not fair that you got kicked from practice too. You didn't do anything." The rest of the team—hell, maybe not even coach—might not realize how hard Nate had been busting his ass to rise in the ranks, but I did.

"Eh, it's not like it really matters." He shrugged like it was nothing, but the defeat in his eyes betrayed him.

I threw an arm around his shoulders. "Fuck that noise. What do you say we get cleaned up and grab some ice cream from town?"

Nate looked at me like I'd lost my fucking mind, which, given my headspace over the last several weeks, wasn't entirely out of the question.

"What? You're rank, man," I said with a straight face.

He barked out a laugh, but thankfully didn't push me off. I definitely would have fallen on my ass. "You're on, but the first round is on you."

"First round? How much ice cream you planning to eat?" I teased.

Rather than answer, he held open the metal door for me. I slid free of his shoulders and made my way inside. It took me a shameful amount of time to get my bruised as fuck body cleaned and dried. But Nate didn't complain or rush me. He could be kind of a nuisance, but he was a real stand-up guy, always had been.

By the time we made it to town, the ache in my chest and back had mostly subsided. The bell over the door to the creamery dinged as we stepped in from the warm afternoon.

"Hello, boys. What'll it be?" the pretty young woman staffing the counter asked. I gestured for Nate to go first, and he didn't hesitate to step forward.

"I'll take a three scoop Neopolitan in a waffle cone, on his tab," he added with a smirk, pointing his thumb back at me.

I frowned as I joined him at the counter. "Really, man? Three scoops? How are you gonna eat all that before it melts?"

He flashed me a self-satisfied grin before walking off with zero shame to grab a drink at the water fountain while his obscene order was being put together.

"Lose a bet?" the young woman asked.

"Something like that. Can I get two scoops of mint chocolate chip in a waffle cone?"

She flashed a pleased smile and her cheeks turned rosy when I returned it. We were probably about the same age. This was likely her afternoon job, which made it unlikely that she attended the all girl's school.

I paid, leaving a hefty tip, and joined Nate at the table he'd claimed with both cones in hand. "Here's your monstrosity."

"It's not a monstrosity, it's a work of art."

I snorted and took a seat. "Whatever happened to committing to a flavor?"

"Neopolitan *is* a flavor," he countered as he tasted the top scoop.

"Maybe, but I don't really think independent scoops of chocolate, vanilla, and strawberry are the same thing."

"That's because you have a limited imagination."

I snorted. My imagination was plenty healthy, hence why the coach had accused me of chasing butterflies at practice…again. If I couldn't stop getting distracted by thoughts of Andy while there was a live ball, then I'd really get hurt instead of just getting my bell rung like earlier.

Nate leaned forward 'til his cone was practically dripping on the table and nodded toward the young woman that had fixed our ice creams. "What do you think of Deborah?"

Was that her name? I hadn't even looked. "She's cute," I said with a shrug. "Why do you ask?"

"I think she recently graduated from the public high school. Seen her around town a bit. She's super nice." Nate stared wistfully at the brunette currently greeting a small family.

"Oh yeah? You like her?" I crunched into a bite of chocolate. Nate and I had talked about girls throughout the years. Though, now that I thought about it, it had been a while. That was probably on me.

He ducked his head and hiked a shoulder. "Maybe. What about you? Now that you're single and all."

I winced inwardly and glanced at the young woman again. She really was cute and clearly every bit as sweet as the ice cream she served. Her brown hair was pulled back in a short bouncy ponytail and her apron hugged her curves in a way that was eye-catching without being lewd or inappropriate. From a purely subjective point of view, she was very attractive, classic girl-next-door, and…not my type in the least. I realized Nate was still waiting for a response and shifted my gaze back to him. "Nah, not really my jam."

Nate smirked. "That's right, she's not a redhead."

I nearly dropped my cone on the floor. "W-what?"

His cheeks tinged a light pink. "Word might have gotten around that the reason Trixie dyed her hair that awful burgundy color was because you said you were into redheads." He tilted his head to the side and considered me. "You were never really into her, were you?"

"Is it that obvious?" I asked with a grimace.

"Not to the rest of the crew, but we've been roommates for four years. You never seemed…excited to meet up with her."

I blanched and tried to hide it behind a giant chomp of ice cream that instantly made my teeth numb. If Nate had noticed that, what else had he noticed?

"Yo, don't worry. If you don't like her like that, then you don't. What I don't get is why you kept dating for so long if you weren't into it, not to mention telling her you prefer redheads."

I sighed and slouched in my chair, abandoning what was left of my ice cream. I had no idea how Nate had managed to go through so much of his. My stomach was churning from all the sugar. "Would you believe me if I said I tried *multiple* times to let her down easy? Everything from saying I didn't have time to date to outright telling her we should be friends. The hair thing was kind of a last ditch effort to get her to get the hint."

"Damn." Nate let out a low whistle. "Wish you'd have said something. I could have helped."

My lips twisted into a dubious frown. "How? By taking her off my hands?"

"Shit, man. No. I'm not an asshole like that," Nate said my forcefully than I expected. "I know I've joked about things in the past, but that was really for the rest of the guys. I wouldn't do that to you. But we could have figured *something* out. You shouldn't have to date someone you don't like just because everyone expects you to."

I swallowed and stared down at the linoleum tabletop. Maybe I should have given Nate more credit over the years, let him in a little more, instead of suffering in silence. "You're a great guy, Nate."

He rolled his eyes. "I know and nice guys always finish last." He scowled at the remnants of his cone before popping it in his mouth.

We stood, and I clasped him on the shoulder. "Not always. Don't do shit to appease the rest of the asshats. You're a good-looking guy and hella nice. Anyone would be lucky to have you. The way you *are*." I glanced over my shoulder to see what the adorable Deborah was doing—wiping down the counter and refilling the toppings. "I'm gonna pop outside and thaw a bit, maybe take a little walk. You go talk to Deborah."

Nate's mouth fell open and his gaze darted uncertainly to the young woman he was clearly crushing hard on. "I don't know if you've noticed, but I'm shit at talking to women."

"Take your time and be yourself. You've got this." I squeezed his shoulder and gave him a wink before making my way back into the sun.

Chapter 15

Andy

I glanced out the window at the stunning afternoon beyond, not paying nearly enough attention to the day's lesson. My gaze wandered over my peers, looking equally bored with Professor Isaac's monotone presentation about the awfulness that was the Twenties. I debated sneaking out one of my own books to read instead. It wouldn't be the first time I feigned absorption in the class text to hide a better book. But alas, Isaac had yet to direct us to a particular page or even to take out the massive history tomb. I slumped in my chair and continued to let my gaze wander, however when I caught sight of a familiar face in the small window of the door, I immediately straightened.

My eyes widened in alarm as Mitch smiled and offered a small wave, then pointed down. I frowned and shook my head slightly. His gaze darted to the professor, whose back was still to the class as he scratched out relevant events on the board and back to me. I did a quick survey of my peers to see if anyone else had noticed our audience, but everyone seemed thoroughly absorbed in their own misery. I brought my gaze back to Mitch and shook my head again. Was he crazy? What was he thinking popping up like that?

His hazel eyes rolled in obvious agitation, and he gestured more forcefully for me to look down. With a frown, I did so to see my expectantly bare desk. I looked back up at him and shrugged in confusion. He threw his hands up, and for a second, I thought he might have a fit right there in the hallway. Then he mimed a lifting motion.

I frowned harder and returned my attention to the desk. It didn't lift to reveal a storage cubby like the ones in the younger classes did. On a whim, I reached under the desk and felt around, praying I didn't encounter something gross. When my fingers found folded paper taped to the underside, my eyes widened in surprise and I glanced over at Mitch, still popping in and out of the window like a loon. He gave me two thumbs up and disappeared again.

I chewed on my bottom lip as I carefully extracted the paper and unfolded it in my lap. With a last look around to make sure no one was paying me any attention, I glanced down at the scribbled note.

Play hooky with me

I stared at the note, reading it several more times, but the four words didn't change. A quick glance at the door showed Mitch hadn't reappeared either. I quickly ran through all the reasons this was a horrible idea. I never skipped class. Except for recent events, I'd barely had a sick day. I couldn't simply walk out in the middle of a lesson. I just...couldn't.

I crumpled the paper and shoved it into my blazer pocket, then my arm went straight into the air. "Professor Isaac?"

The professor turned around and looked at me over his glasses. "Yes, Mr. Gallagher? Did you have a question?"

"No sir. I'm actually not feeling well and was wondering if I could be excused." Anxiety tightened around my chest at the bald-faced lie.

"I hope it's nothing too serious."

"I don't think so. Maybe just low blood sugar," I offered, already starting to wuss out.

To my amazement, Isaac nodded and gestured toward the door. "See that you take better care of yourself in the future, young man. Growing bodies need nourishment. As a matter of fact," he began as he turned back toward the board to resume the lesson.

I quickly scooped up my satchel and zipped out of the room before he could change his mind. Out in the hall, I shook my head and settled the bag more securely around me. "I can't believe that worked."

"What excuse did you use?"

I nearly leapt out of my skin. "Why do you always have to sneak up on me?"

He scoffed. "It's hardly sneaking if you already knew I was out here. It's not my fault you can't see what's in front of your own nose." I stuck my tongue out at him and he chuckled quietly. "Come on, let's drop your bag off and get you changed."

"What? Why?" I asked, suddenly realizing that Mitch wasn't in his school uniform, but in light denim and a faded green tee. My gaze rebelliously latched onto where the thin fabric stretched across his chest and my fingers buzzed with desire to reach out and smooth the wrinkled fabric. I jerked back to awareness as he divested me of my satchel.

"First, dropping off this monstrosity," he said as he slung the heavy bag over his own shoulder, "means you don't have to lug it around. Second, having it in your room will make it more believable that you've only stepped out for a minute. As for changing, it'd be pretty fucking conspicuous for us to be wandering around town in uniforms when we're supposed to be in class."

"We're going to town?"

"You have a better idea?" Mitch countered as he started walking toward the east dormitories. I faltered, momentarily surprised that he knew where my room was. Then I remembered he'd been there before. By the time I finally got my feet moving, he'd made it nearly all the way to the adjoining hall, walking like he didn't have a care in the world. I raced to catch up with him and he glanced over at me, humor dancing in his eyes right beside the mischief.

"Shut up. You know I don't skip."

"Didn't say anything," he said with a teasing smile that belied his words.

"You were thinking it."

"I'll have to keep better tabs on my thoughts if you've become a mind reader." He tossed me a crooked grin and turned the corner. I followed beside him and couldn't help but wonder what thoughts Mitch could possibly be worried about me reading.

Mitch

I couldn't say why I was shocked to discover Andy owned jeans, but I most definitely was, and skinny jeans to boot. They clung to his legs, outlining muscles with every step he took. He surged a couple paces ahead of me as my own steps slowed to appreciate how his equally fitted dark teal shirt shaped his back and stopped shy of his tight ass.

Stop thinking about Andy's tight ass.

Despite the order, my gaze lingered on the captured globes. Fuck, Andy looked good in jeans. Everyone knew that the school uniform wasn't doing anyone any favors, but this was a fucking crime. Suddenly, the ass I was not supposed to be staring at like some depraved lecher stopped moving. I quickly jerked my attention to somewhere safer, which happened to be a chalkboard sign on the sidewalk.

"You alright? What are you thinking about?"

Peeling you out of those tight pants and spanking that perfect ass until it burns red.

I blinked in alarm at the unexpected conclusion of the wicked thought. What was it about Andy that brought out the animal in me? Was it the air of innocence he still possessed even now, though I knew he was far from it? Was it that he was almost a year younger? Or was it me? Maybe I really was just a base animal that couldn't control himself.

"Hello. Earth to Mitch. Do you read me?" I blinked again to find Andy standing right in front of me, his auburn hair shining like the purest copper in the sunlight and his expressive emeralds flashing with humor.

"What? Yeah. I was just..." My gaze darted past him to the sign. "Reading." His eyes squinted as he frowned and I gestured behind him. "Isn't that the bookstore you used to sneak off to all the time?"

He twisted around to look and then turned back, his face morphing into shock. "You remember?"

There were a lot of things that I remembered, especially where Andy was concerned. I remembered how he hated carrots with a fiery passion of a thousand suns and how he believed that smoked

Gouda was superior among cheese while Havarti could rot. I remembered how animated he got when plotting a prank or talking about his family. I remembered how his lips tasted and how his body seemed to fit my hands perfectly. I remembered how he always made me feel like a person, like I was enough.

I didn't say any of that, though. Instead, I smirked and said, "Of course." A smile that could light even the darkest room stretched across his face. "Also, it's literally the only bookstore in town."

His smile flipped into a scowl, and he popped me in the arm. "Just for that, we're going in."

Laughter bubbled out of me as he grabbed my arm and dragged me into the small shop crowded with every kind of book imaginable. "Okay, we're in," I said when he finally released me between two leaning towers of paperbacks.

"Oh, no you don't. We're not leaving until *you* get a book."

I shook my head. "I'm not a great reader like you, Andy. What good would a book do me?"

"Why do you do that?"

"Do what?" I asked as I plucked at a worn cover nearby.

"Belittle yourself."

"I do not," I scoffed, moving my attention to another frayed edge. His hand covered the fingers worrying the binding, and I met his steady gaze.

"Yes, you do. You're not dumb, Mitch. I keep telling you that. Maybe one day you'll believe it. As for what a book could do for you, books are an escape, a way to be someone else, even if it's only for a little while."

I curled my fingers inward, but his hand stayed over mine, his thumb absently stroking my wrist. My pulse pounded faster at the minute contact. Was it possible Andy really could read minds?

That he already knew all the things I was too scared to say out loud?

He gave my hand a light squeeze and raised his eyebrows. "Still like sci-fi?"

I nodded without thinking as I leaned forward. This moment certainly felt like fiction and I'd do just about anything to keep it going. Andy's full lips quirked up in a soft smile and quickly became the only thing I could see. The thousands of books around us vanished, the musky scent of old paper and dust gone to be replaced entirely by Andy's herbal scent and the sensuous curve of his mouth.

"Come on." He squeezed my hand again, and I blinked to find the world once more as it should be.

I let out a sigh as the fantasy slipped through my fingers.

Andy nudged me in the ribs, his smile still bright and completely oblivious to my inner turmoil. Guess he couldn't read minds after all. If he could, maybe this wouldn't feel so fucking impossible. "Don't be like that. This place may not have the largest selection of literature, but I'm sure we'll find you something you'll enjoy." I smiled back at him—though I doubted it reached my eyes—and let him lead me deeper into the cavern of words.

An hour later, he did indeed find a book I found interesting enough to read about space pirates…because, well, fucking space pirates. We stepped up to the counter and he placed down not one, but five books.

"Really, Andy," I said as he added a tote with an image of a dragon curled around a hoard of books.

"What? I can't come to a bookstore and not very well buy a book. And we need something to carry them in since *someone* made me leave my satchel at the school."

"Well, *someone* carries too many things in said satchel. There wouldn't have been room anyway."

He snorted and thanked the cashier before shoving the receipt into the bag. Then he slung it over his shoulder, looking quite pleased with himself. "There's always room for books." He took a step toward the exit and I suddenly realized I had no idea where *my* book had gone.

"Shit."

"What's the matter?" he asked, his hand already on the door.

"I don't know where I put my book. Damn it, I actually really wanted to read that."

A smile brightened his whole face, and he patted his new bag. "I've got it."

"But… You didn't have to do that."

He shrugged and finished pushing the door open. "I wanted to. Besides, that's what friends are for, right?"

I floated in a haze of wonder as I trailed after him back into the lazy afternoon. Andy had actually called us friends, something I'd never thought to hear him say again after the horrible mess I'd made of our friendship. I was definitely reading that fucking book now.

Chapter 16

Mitch

I made my way down the hall scattered with the occasional student. Most of the school had taken advantage of the half-day to venture into town or catch up on assignments, leaving the walkways mostly abandoned. That suited me just fine. Pretending that I cared about the same things most of them did was getting harder every day. So what if Trixie was dating Ronald Harrington? Who cared that the lacrosse schedule had been rearranged or that the school board of trustees had their quarterly meeting coming up? Not me.

The hall turned and opened up to a larger passage. My pace quickened. I didn't want to be late for my study session with Andy, and I'd stupidly left my bag in my room. I may have done well on my midterms, but seasons weren't won by giving up on practice after winning one key game. Not to mention, I enjoyed my time with Andy. It was the rare occasion that I could actually be myself, that I didn't have to pretend. He didn't expect me to be perfect and didn't judge me when I struggled. The routine we'd fallen into mostly wasn't awkward as long as I didn't think about certain things and kept my hands to myself.

The adjoining hall that led to the dormitories came into view, and my stride lengthened. To my horror, Brian stepped out of the wing flanked by John, Kyle, and, of course, Nate. I cursed inwardly and nearly tripped. Brian's gaze roved the almost vacant hallway until it rested on me. His eyes narrowed, and he stalked forward, not at all his usual, easygoing self.

"Hey guys, what's up?" I asked as I forced my feet to keep moving forward instead of turning around and sprinting as fast as possible in the opposite direction, notes be damned. The group walked up the middle of the hall, blocking my original path. I veered to the side to go around. As one, the group shifted to cut me off once more.

"I'll tell you what's up. Where the fuck have you been?" Brian asked, his finger jabbing at me in the air.

I swallowed and took an involuntary step closer to the wall. "What do you mean? I've been here."

"You've been blowing off practice," Kyle said, his enormous arms crossed menacingly over his chest. As the school's starting goalie, Kyle really wasn't someone you wanted to be on the wrong side of.

"They aren't formal practices," I argued.

John scoffed. "You know as well as we do that doesn't mean shit as far as Coach is concerned. Practice is mandatory, formal or not."

"Excuse the fuck out of me for giving a shit about my grades," I snapped. Nate opened his mouth to—I hoped—back me up, but Brian held up a hand to cut him off before he got so much as a sound out.

"Since when is studying a priority? You've never shown any interest in it before. Why now?"

"Things are different." The truth about not wanting to play anymore sat on the tip of my tongue. But much as it burned in me to confess everything, I couldn't do it. Too much was at stake to take the risk.

"Different like how?" John asked, a scowl etched into his sunburned face.

"If you're worried about having grades good enough to get accepted to college, the scouts don't care. The school will take care of it," Nate offered in a way that I imagined he found helpful.

"Maybe I'm tired of the school taking care of everything. Is it so wrong to want to earn it on my own?"

"Yeah, it fucking is." Brian stepped forward and pushed me. I stumbled back into the wall and stared at him in shock. Brian and I were close, or as close as anyone on the team really was.

"What the fuck?" I moved to sidestep the lot of them, only to have Kyle cut off my escape with his imposing frame.

"You're not the only one on the team, Hudson. Don't dick this up for the rest of us," Kyle rumbled.

I let out an aggravated huff and directed my response to Brian, who was clearly in charge of this little intervention. "Look, I'll be at practice today, okay? Satisfied? Now, move, I have somewhere to be."

Brian placed a hand on my chest and forced me back against the wall. A growl slipped free before I could rein it in. He dropped his arm, but not the glower. "Not good enough. You need to fucking show up. None of this half-assed playing bullshit. You're our lead Attackman. Act like it."

"Fine, whatever."

"You're not hearing me. Either you get your shit together or we'll be having this chat with your faggot tutor."

My jaw. "Don't talk about Andy like that. You know he's off limits."

"Not anymore," Kyle said, taking up a position beside Brian. "Consider your standing blanket of protection for that pillow-biter stripped. The fag is fair game."

White-hot rage burned through me, getting hotter with each word. "You don't fucking touch him."

"What are you going to do about?" Brian glanced at the others, who all mirrored his sneer. "How do you think that pansy-ass, fucking queer—"

My fist hit Brian's jaw mid-slur.

He stumbled back and looked up at me, clutching the side of his face. "You son of a motherfucking bitch!" He launched himself at me. Unfortunately, I didn't get my hands up in time to prevent his own fist from slamming into my face. Stars exploded in my vision and all reasonable thought went up in smoke.

I pushed off the wall and caught Brian in the middle hard enough to send us both crashing to the ground. We scrabbled for the upper hand, pushing, pulling, and hitting whatever we could reach. Hands ripped at my shirt and arms until a hit from Brian sent me flying. I raced to get back on my feet, only to have John and Kyle crash into me while Brian regained his own footing.

Brian wiped at his mouth and looked at the blood on his fingers before stepping up to rejoin the others. "You'll pay for that. Thought we were friends." John moved aside and Brian's fist landed squarely in my gut.

I clutched my middle and met him glare for glare. "Go fuck yourself."

Nate stepped forward and inserted himself between us. "Stop. This has gone too far. We're going to get expelled and then no one plays."

Brian fingered his jaw again. "No, we won't." He shoved Nate out of the way and pulled back his arm again.

Andy

I followed the noise until I turned a corner and found the source. Nathaniel stumbled back as Brian pushed him out of the way to get to Mitch. Both of their faces twisted into snarls as they slammed into each other with enough force to make me flinch. John and Kyle leapt in to join the fray, clearly eager to get their licks in. Without a second thought, I dropped my bag and sprinted toward them. My feet skidded across the floor with a horrible screech as I came to an abrupt halt and slammed into John. He flew back, and I spun to face Kyle just in time to get socked in the mouth.

I tasted the metallic tang of what was undoubtedly a split lip and clocked Kyle right back. The shock on his face before he fell was well worth any reprisal I might endure. A glance over at John revealed he was well on his way to regaining his bearings. Meanwhile, Brian and Mitch were in a free for all of swinging fists, rolling on the ground. Nathaniel spun to confront me. Instead of waiting to find out what he would do, I barreled into him with my full weight. While not much compared to his, it was sufficient. Not expecting the hit, he fell hard into Brian, who'd just come out on top. The two crashed to the ground in a heap of angry limbs, shoving at each other and spitting curses.

Mitch scrambled to his feet then immediately began advancing on Brian, unadulterated rage sparking in his eyes. I caught his arm, and he looked down at me. He blinked, and the fury clouding his vision gave way to surprise. "Andy? What are you doing here?"

"Saving your dumb ass. Come on, let's go." I tugged on his arm.

He stumbled a couple of steps, then pulled back as he looked around at the others. "But—"

"But, nothing. We need to get out of here before any of the faculty shows up." I yanked harder on his arm and he fell into a lurching run. We sprinted through the dormitories, which were mercifully empty, until we skidded up to a side exit.

"Where are you going? They'll just find us again." Mitch panted beside me, hands on his knees, casting furtive glances down the twist of hallways we'd navigated.

"Trust me. I know a place." My fingers brushed the hidden key at the top of the doorjamb as I winked at him. I quickly used it to open the exit. Sunlight poured through the opening, momentarily blinding me. I stashed the key back where I'd found it and dragged Mitch through the opening. He hesitated, and I rolled my eyes. "It automatically locks. Now, come on."

Not a soul watched us slip out of the dorms or skirt along the outer buildings or even bolt across the quarter mile of open terrain. Few had any reason to venture this far north of the campus. Well, few without illicit intents. I smiled as I spied our destination lurking on the edge of the woods. The forgotten shack held a plethora of discarded junk from the school, everything from canoes and nets for a lake commandeered by the township a decade ago to outdated sports equipment from the seventies.

"How did you find this place?" Mitch asked, turning in a circle as he gawked at all the stuff.

I moved over to one of the grime covered windows and shifted a moth-eaten sheet to allow a ray of dim light into the otherwise dreary room. "You're not the only one who finds neat places." Truthfully, Connor had found it, then shared it with me while we'd been dating. It was the perfect spot to get lost for a few hours without worrying about someone showing up unexpectedly.

Mitch glanced over at me like he wanted to ask another question, but returned his attention to the room at large instead. "This place is freaking ancient."

"Been here at least forty years." I squatted down and swiped a finger along the dusty floor. "Better news, no one has been here for a while. They won't think to look for us here. I doubt they even know it exists."

"That's a relief." There was a brief pause, and then, "Fuck."

I looked up at the expletive and found Mitch plucking at his ripped shirt. My gaze traveled up his long torso to his mouth twisted into a frown and the rest of the damage that had been done to him. Brushing my hands off, I stood and walked over. "You gonna tell me what all that was about?"

Mitch's shoulders stiffened and his gaze darted off to the side. It seemed like that would be the only answer I'd get when he broke the silence. "The team isn't happy about how much practice I've been missing."

I frowned. "Okay, but it's not like you're skipping for the hell of it. You're studying."

"They don't see it that way." His shoulders sagged. The heavy air of defeat around him hurt my heart.

"I don't get it. If they're so fucking awful, why do you stay? Just quit the team. No one deserves to be treated like that."

He let out a cynical laugh and lifted his gaze to meet mine. "If only it were that easy."

I wanted to argue that it was. All he had to do was walk away. He wouldn't be alone. He'd have me. But the sheer level of sadness swimming in his eyes held my tongue. "You're gonna have one hell of a shiner," I said instead, indicating Mitch's face. A little closer and I could actually touch him. I fought back the impulse to do exactly that and dropped my hand even as he raised his, and took a step back.

He flinched as he touched the quickly purpling bruise on his cheek, dangerously close to his eye. Even in the gloom, it was easy to tell the bruise would be massive. "You didn't get off so unscathed yourself," he commented in return.

"What do you mean?" I asked, stopping my retreat.

He took a step closer, shrinking the distance I'd opened between us, and reached out. His thumb brushed lightly along my bottom lip. A jolt of electric pain shot through me at the contact. He took another half step closer, all but eliminating the meager distance remaining. His brow furrowed, as if he was inspecting the damage. "Looks like it hurts," he whispered.

My mouth parted slightly as his thumb traced the path again. I wanted to tell him it didn't hurt, but wasn't sure I trusted myself to speak. Not when he was so close and all I could think about was how good his hands felt. Then his lips closed on mine, harsh and needy. His insistence swallowed the resulting sharp lance of pain as the force re-split my lip. I didn't care. Any pain was worth enduring if it meant I could have Mitch like this. Desperately, or maybe stupidly, I kissed him back every bit as feverishly. The heady mix of pain and pleasure making me higher than I already was.

Suddenly, he pulled away, our lips sticking together until the last possible second. My heart raced even as my breaths got shallower. Every cell in my body zeroed in on him, inexplicably and perfectly in tune with his every movement.

His eyes widened, and he dropped his hand as if finally realizing what he'd done. "I'm sorry, I…" he stuttered.

"Take it off," I ordered.

"Take what off?"

"All of it," I said, and eliminated the distance. My mouth closed over his like I planned to suck the very essence of him out while my fingers set to work eliminating his ruined shirt.

He shrugged his shoulders back as I forced the material off of him. The shirt fell to the floor with a muffled thump. I expected him to argue like he had when I'd gotten to my knees, but he didn't. He separated from my mouth long enough to pull his undershirt over his head and kick off his shoes while I tackled his pants.

My fingers touched bare skin and my mind went utterly blank. All that existed was the warmth suffusing my hand as I ran it up his torso. I was touching Mitch. Finally, after all this time. Logic struggled back to the forefront and brought with it caution. Already I was losing myself in him. I mentally shook myself out of the fog that had swallowed me.

Control. I can do this if I stay in control.

Chapter 17

Mitch

Andy grabbed my arm for the fifth time that afternoon and dragged me around a pile of junk. On the other side, the space was remarkably clear and dominated by a makeshift cot. Andy fluffed the sheet and a cloud of dust went up. I fanned the motes out of my face and was rewarded with the vision of Andy finally stripping his own clothes off. I suppressed a groan and hated how hard I was just at the promise of touching his bare skin.

He kicked away his pants, then stepped close to yank me down for another searing kiss. My hands automatically went around his waist, but he stepped back again before I could crush him against me.

"Where the fuck did I put it?" he mumbled to himself as he searched along some cluttered shelves. "Ah-ha." He pulled out a small bottle, then promptly flipped it over to read something on the bottom. Then he checked a string a square foils. How he could read anything in this gloom was beyond me, but it didn't stop him from concluding, "Still good. Perfect." He set it back down within easy reach of the odd pallet. I pushed away all thoughts about why this cot, a bottle of lube, and condoms would be here—or how

Andy would know about them—and focused on the only thing that mattered right then. This was actually happening.

I stepped back in close and caught his face so I could steal another kiss. Even after all this time, Andy still had the softest lips I'd ever tasted. I hungrily snatched at them, mindless of what that could say about me. My hand ran down his side while I shifted my focus to his neck. He let out a soft moan and shuddered. My hand continued to rove until it rounded over his ass. I pressed him against me and a groan rose from my throat, deep and almost feral.

He yanked back, the sound of our combined harsh breathing filling the otherwise silent space. His eyes practically burned as he took in every inch of me from head to toe. "Hands and knees."

I took a whole step forward before I faltered. Had I heard that right? He caught the hesitation, but didn't move.

"You can say no, and this is as far as this goes."

I blinked, still struggling to process the unexpected development, and searched his face while my mind ran a veritable gauntlet. Could I do this? Could I really bottom for Andy?

His face softened. "You don't have to do anything you don't want to. All you have to do is say the word."

Consent. He was asking for consent. Exactly what I should have done four years ago. I swallowed hard and stepped closer, my mind already made up. "Okay." I leaned forward and swiped my mouth against his, the sharp tang of metal from the split in his lip grounding me.

I can do this.

Without another word, I did exactly as he'd instructed and got on my hands and knees. Embarrassment warred with doubt as I felt him move behind me. I told them both to shut the fuck up and tried to relax.

He placed a hand on my hip, and I flinched. "I promise I won't hurt you. You can stop this anytime. No questions. No guilt. We walk away like it never happened."

I seriously doubted that last was evenly remotely possible given how far things had already gone, but even if it was true, I had no intention of backing out now. I glanced over my shoulder at him. He knelt behind me every bit as naked as I, his red hair blazing in the thin ray of light he'd let in earlier. A tightness in my chest loosened. That was enough. "I trust you."

He leaned forward to snag a quick kiss, his body pressing against mine as he laid across my back to reach my mouth. All too soon, though, the skin to skin I ached for was gone.

I dropped my head between my shoulders and worked on not freaking the fuck out about what was about to happen. It couldn't be all bad, right? I wasn't dumb. Plenty of guys bottomed. It was normal; it was balance; it was... A slick finger slid delicately over my hole and I yelped in surprise.

"Sorry, should have warned you it'd be a little cold." He chuckled, but didn't remove his hand. Truth was, the temperature had little to do with it, and it didn't hurt, it felt...nice? "Remember, all you have to do is say the word."

I nodded, and it turned out that was my warning as he slowly worked his slim finger inside.

My entire body rebelled at the intrusion, even my shoulders clenched and my fingers white-knuckled in the sheet. I focused on my breathing and worked through convincing each muscle to relax. It didn't hurt exactly; it was just weird, and I felt exposed, like

I was on display. My cheeks burned and suddenly I was grateful Andy couldn't see my face.

"There you go," Andy whispered as he deliberately moved his finger in and out, ratcheting up the weirdness to a million.

When he added another, I almost called it quits, promise to myself or not. Then he pressed all the way in and curled his fingers as if looking for something. I was about to ask him what the fuck he expected to find when pleasure hummed through me like someone had hit a bell. A moan nearly choked me, and Andy chuckled again.

"*That* is called your prostate." He stroked it again just as gently, and my cock twitched back to life. "You're welcome."

"Are you planning to give me anatomy lessons the whole time?" I panted as he continued to methodically work me open, ensuring to show attention to the treasure he'd found.

"Would it help?" The laughter on the edge of his voice spread a warmth through me I hadn't expected.

Fuck me, yeah, it probably would.

I was about to tell him as much when he removed his fingers. Never in a million years would I have thought I'd actually miss them. Then something decidedly not an index finger pressed against my hole and I shot straight back to panic. He worked his way in with slow, shallow thrusts like he had with his fingers, and I worked on the same process of forcing myself to calm the fuck down. Behind me, Andy's ragged breathing mirrored my own and guilt surged through me. Had he been this freaked when I...

He slid deeper suddenly, and I nearly choked at the incredible fullness of having all of him. "We can stop," he said softly as he held perfectly still.

My thoughts whirled in a million directions until they all circled one. *I can do this.* "No," I finally croaked, then immediately panicked again when I realized how that might sound. "Keep going."

His hands stroked lightly up my sides as far as his reach would allow and flowed their way back down, tracing every minute outline of muscle I had as if following a map. The anxiety coiled in my chest eased again and I let out a breath. That. I needed Andy to touch me, ground me, remind me it was him.

"Curiosity killed the cat," Andy whispered.

I took another deep breath. "Satisfaction brought it back."

His thumbs stroked over the dimples in my back. "Tell me when you're ready." The thoughtful check-in only served to further highlight the differences between this and all of my other experiences. Andy may not like it, but he cared. He was still my best friend, and that was all I needed.

"Okay. I'm good."

His rhythm started slow and purposeful. Thankfully, I didn't tense up again and the foreign sensation settled into an interesting buildup of pressure. An odd sort of good I hadn't expected. He sank all the way in and on the backstroke, adjusted his hips. I gasped as his ensuing thrusts stroked over my prostate again and again. Andy's pants filled my ears, joining my own as well as a moan. Because fuck, that felt good.

"Give me your hand."

I didn't even think, just adjusted my balance and did as he said. He took it and guided it to my outrageously hard dick where his fingers wrapped around mine. The groan that fell out of me wasn't even human as I tightened my hold, and fuck, if Andy guiding my hand didn't instantly become the single most erotic moment of my life. My entire body stiffened as my orgasm hit me with the same surprise everything else had.

"Shit. Fuck," Andy hissed. Then he was gone and my ass was left clenching nothing. I moaned at the awful ache of emptiness while Andy's heavy breathing increased until he grunted and his own release splattered across my back. I dropped my hand to the ground before I could fall over from the head rush.

Andy

I stayed fixed to the ground for a solid minute, as if roots had sprouted from my knees and sunk through the layers of flooring and earth. Gradually, my breathing returned to normal, and I blinked away the last of my post-orgasm fog. The splatters of cum across Mitch's back stood out in stark contrast to his tan skin, and my stomach twisted.

Check on him. I need to check on him.

Despite knowing what I needed to do, those weren't the words that came out of my mouth as I stood on shaking legs and kicked the used condom out of sight. "Give me a second to find a towel or something. Don't move."

"Fuck that," he grumbled, and promptly rolled away from his own mess to lie on his back. He let out a sigh and closed his eyes without glancing over at me. The insecurity I thought long since buried reared its head as if its grave had been a shallow one instead of the deepest pit I could dig. My gaze kept sliding over the rumpled sheets to the evidence of Mitch's release.

Why did I think this was a good idea? Why didn't he call my bluff?

"That was…different."

My gaze flicked back to Mitch's face. He blinked at the ceiling, then turned his head to look at me. I braced myself for the worst. When I wanted to break something, I really went all fucking out. "Bad different?"

His mouth didn't curve into a smile, but it seemed to shine in his eyes. "No. Just…different."

I shakily released the death grip on my anxiety and extended a hand to help him up. "We should probably get going before it gets too late." His strong fingers wrapped around my forearm and my heart thudded hard at the feel of his hands on me.

"Yeah. And I have a practice I have to get to."

"You can't be serious." He snorted in response and I fought the urge to shake my head in disbelief, or better, argue. How could he possibly want to go to that stupid practice after what his team-mates had done? After what we'd done? Sure, the fight had been about his missing practice, but surely his black eye was reason enough to skip, not to mention how uncomfortable he'd be.

He straightened up, and though he tried to hide it, I caught the twinge of discomfort. I'd prepped him as much as possible, but all the prepping in the world couldn't account for the sheer newness, that ache of emptiness after being so full.

I miss that.

I ruthlessly crushed the rogue yearning. I didn't bottom, not anymore, not for a long time. Of course, losing control like I had today also wasn't something I ever did either. Mitch released my arm, and I bent to grab my clothes from the floor. Doubt continued to ricochet inside me as he walked around the barrier meant to obscure the cot from anyone that might happen by to retrieve his ruined uniform. I focused on setting myself to rights before joining him. At the vision of Mitch's sculpted back, though, my fingers faltered on the last few of my shirt buttons as they remembered what he'd felt like beneath them. *Warm, hard yet pliable…mine.* I shook off the thoughts and forced my fingers back to their task, then found my shoes.

"Probably a good thing they'll bench you after what happened," I said to distract myself.

"They won't."

I glanced up at his deadpan response, but he still had his back to me. A surge of worry snuffed out my rampant anxiety. I finished tying my shoe and stood. "Then I suggest you find some way to sit out."

Mitch turned and gave me one of the saddest looks I'd ever seen mar his beautiful face. "You know I can't do that, *especially* after the fight."

All of my doubts about what we'd done officially took a backseat to my concern for his wellbeing. He'd said before that he didn't want to play anymore, had dropped countless clues over the last several weeks, but only now was I finally getting the full picture of what these last four years had done to him. The tightness around his eyes spoke of an exhaustion that had nothing to do with the physical. The slump of his shoulders stood testament to a wariness that came from being beaten down constantly. Was it possible that I was the only person in Mitch's life that actually saw any of this? That cared?

"Mitch."

He sighed and stepped closer. I was so busy searching his face, the sudden press of his lips against mine took me by surprise. Where the kiss before had been borderline manic in its fervor, this one was slow and purposeful. It wrapped gently around my heart and called to the deepest parts of me that seemed to exist sole-ly for him. When Mitch pulled away, he took a part of me with him. I licked my lips, tasting him there, along with a longing I didn't dare entertain.

"You could always pretend to be sick. I've got an excellent trick for that."

He laughed quietly and touched his forehead briefly against mine before leaning back. "Thank you for caring."

My heart twisted in my chest at the unwitting confirmation of my suspicion that no one was looking out for Mitch. "That's what friends do."

"You're right." His hazel eyes glowed with the same small smile that tugged at his lips. "You're right."

"I'm usually right."

He laughed softly again as he trailed the backs of his fingers along my cheek, then dropped his hand. "Okay, smarty pants, know a way out of here that doesn't land us in hot water?"

I offered him a crooked smile and stepped past him to the back wall. "Is that a real question, or are you actually doubting me?" I asked with raised eyebrows as I pushed open the nearly invisible back door. Beyond, the dense foliage of a forest un-willing to give up its evergreen crowded up to the shack.

"You sly bastard," he said in awe as he approached the open doorway and the late afternoon light.

I gestured to our left at a narrow path that hugged the build-ing and disappeared into the tree line. "If you head that way, you'll end up at the Green in about half a mile. I'll go the opposite way and circle back to the dorm. Or…" I trailed off, not sure how willing I was to tempt this unusual easiness we'd stumbled upon.

Mitch stepped in close while I floundered, invading my personal bubble once again. I fought the urge to swallow and betray the nerves his presence caused me while my heart struggled to find its normal rhythm. "Or," he prompted.

"Or we could walk straight ahead together and…" *And never look back.* "And then part in three-quarters of a mile. That would put you at the practice field sooner."

Mitch looked back at me with those startling perceptive eyes, his lips hovering centimeters away from mine. "And where will that leave you?"

As much a fool for you as I've always been.

I swallowed down the honesty, giving way to my anxiety at last. "I'm not worried about me."

We stared at each other for a moment that stretched into eternity, then Mitch took a step back and looked away. "I don't want to risk it."

The words were like ice water being dumped over my head. Of course not. The whole point was to not get caught together. Taking the alternative path just to steal a few extra minutes together was stupid, reckless. I nodded and took a step toward the winding path that extended in the opposite direction of Mitch's destination.

"Andy."

My traitorous heart hammered against my ribs as I looked back at him over my shoulder.

"I…" He hesitated, then seemed to change his mind. "Be careful. I'll see you tomorrow at lunch," he finished, then turned and settled into a slow jog. I watched him go until the sweep of branches completely obscured him.

Chapter 18

Mitch

Andy was right. I should have skipped practice, and it had absolutely nothing to do with the sting in my ass. *That* I could work with. What I couldn't was the way the team watched every move I made as I stepped into the locker room. Brian especially gave me such a withering expression that my skin should have blistered. Much like mine, parts of his face were swollen, and Kyle and John didn't look any better, though I couldn't recall ever hitting Kyle. Maybe I had. The whole fight was a blur.

I glanced toward the far end of the locker room where, mercifully, fewer people were staring at me like I was an ant under a microscope. As promised, the walk here had been relatively short, but it had been long enough for all the aches and pains to truly set in. I wanted a shower something fierce—for hot water to pummel relaxation into my sore muscles. Considering how much my ribs hurt, I was a little surprised Andy hadn't remarked on any other obvious bruises. But a shower would be weird. No matter that I still had dried blood on my cheekbone.

I took a deep breath that my ribs instantly protested and made my way to my locker. A few of the guys went back to getting ready

175

for practice as I peeled off my ripped shirt with care. I was focusing on not falling over when Kyle's voice boomed loud next to my ear.

"Where's your twink-ass little friend?"

I glanced at him in confusion. First off, Andy wasn't a twink and Kyle calling him one told me he'd never actually *seen* a real twink. Second, why the fuck would Andy be in the lacrosse locker rooms? Before I could find any words, though, Brian cut in.

"You've got some balls, Hudson." Not an uncommon phrase for this group, but normally it was followed by rowdy cheers and ribbing. Brian's face had yet to lose the scowl and his voice had a definite note of challenge.

I reached into the locker, ignoring the pain that lanced across my side, and grabbed the armless tank. Brian's face continued to darken as I pulled it over my head, then reached for my shorts. "Would have thought you'd be pleased. After all, my *balls* are here."

Brian's lip curled while John tried to hide a snort of laughter behind a cough. "You're damn right they are. And you'll keep them here or—"

I finished adjusting the drawstring on my shorts and cut a look at Brian. "Or what? You gonna find a new attackman that can score like I can? You gonna convince coach to let Hendricks start? Tell me, what the fuck are you gonna do, Brian?"

He narrowed his eyes at me and dropped his voice. "You can't watch him twenty-four-seven, Mitch. You so much as show up late for one practice and our next...*conversation* will be with Gallagher."

My throat stuck as I fought the urge to swallow hard. When had my friends gotten so violent? Had they always been this way, and I'd just been too out of it to notice?

"But, Daniels, I wanted to get some payback on that fire crotch," Kyle griped as he rubbed his jaw. I did a double take. *Andy* had done that to Kyle's face? Shit, I needed to give him a high five…and probably make sure he hadn't split his knuckles.

Brian continued to glare at me as he answered our whiny companion, "And you'll have it." Kyle was on his way to a full-out celebration when Brian held up a hand and cut his gaze to him. "The second Hudson stops being a team player. Understood?" he finished, making sure I realized the question was for me as well.

"Ugh." Kyle groaned like it was the worst news he'd received all year. "Yeah, yeah, I get it. Little shit gets to keep his face the way it is…for now." Still grumbling to himself, Kyle walked off, leaving me with Brian and John, who still hadn't moved or spoken since he'd propped a shoulder on the locker beside me.

Brian's hard stare bored into me until I nodded. Then the grim line of his lips flipped into a grin and he clapped me on the shoulder. I nearly dropped from the sheer shock of the one-eighty. "You've got a hell of a right hook on you, Hudson. Let's see if we can't put it to better use on the field." He squeezed my shoulder a hair tighter than normal, then gestured for John to follow him. "See you out there."

I waited until most of the team had filtered out of the locker rooms before sagging against my locker. The cool metal on my back didn't do shit for the sting behind my eyes or the tightness in my chest. Not a one of my teammates had batted an eye as Brian and Kyle blatantly threatened bodily harm to Andy. Not a one had moved to interfere or stop them from cornering me. I don't know what I'd been expecting, but clearly my belief that we had each others' backs was a delusion. This wasn't a team, this was a cult. I bent down to slip on my sneakers, painfully aware of how tight my body had become. I'd been so close to escaping, to finding happiness, but if I put even a toe out of line, it wouldn't be my ass they came for.

I straightened and shook out the tension threatening to pull me under. Andy's worried face from the shack filled my vision and determination burned in my veins. "I can do this. I can be the person they want *and* fix our friendship. I won't be forced to choose, not again."

"Hudson, who are you talking to? And what the hell happened to your face?" Coach Santinelli asked as he exited his office.

"No one. Nothing, sir," I replied quickly.

He squinted at me a moment. "Good, then get your ass out there and start running suicides. And while you're at it, have Hendricks and Bellwether join you."

I kept my groan to myself and gave him a sharp nod. "Yes, sir." Then I turned on my heel and jogged out of the locker rooms to give the others the bad news.

Andy

The public library was more populated than I'd expected, but the constant sound of people searching for books and whispering was oddly comforting. I made a mental note to come by more often. While Ulwich's library might be more grand, the town library had a significantly better selection of fiction and horror, not to mention fewer people who wanted to make my life a living hell.

I glanced at the stack of books I'd checked out about half an hour before in complete disregard of the TBR pile waiting for me at the dorm. The plan had been to read at the little table I'd se-cured by one of the tempered glass windows while I waited for Calvin to finish at the church, but I hadn't so much as cracked a single book. Instead, I kept replaying the events of the last couple of weeks.

I still couldn't get over how...*normal* lunch with Mitch had been. He'd let me top him and the next time we'd seen each other it hadn't been weird or strained, or tense, though I was dying to know how he'd got through practice. If I'd been braver, I might have found a secluded spot to watch the practice for myself, but I'd gone straight back to my room where I'd wor-ried myself sick. And yet, lunch had been normal, our study sessions continued to *be* normal. But I couldn't wrap my head around how. What was I missing? There had to be something. Something staring me in the face. But what?

"Fancy meeting you here," Calvin said as he dropped into an empty chair across from me. He unwound a fancy blue scarf from around his neck. I'd never gotten into fashion or fabrics, but knowing Calvin, it was probably cashmere. He set it beside him, but left his light jacket on. Fall had turned crisp without much warning, unless you took into account that it did that every year around the end of October. Finally, after all the production, he pushed his curls out of his face and leaned forward to rest on his forearms. "Been here long?"

I gave him a wry expression. "Don't pretend like you aren't hoping that I'm ready to go."

He placed all ten fingertips against his chest. "Moi?"

"You can save the act. I'm all set," I said as I reached for the bag holding my latest acquisitions.

"Oh, thank God, I'm starved."

I chuckled as he wrapped the scarf he'd literally just taken off back around his neck in a double loop. "Work up an appetite with all that confessing?" I teased.

"You have *no* idea." Where I'd expected his usual theatric flare, he actually sounded sincere.

I hesitated with the strap over my shoulder, but the weight of the bag still resting on the mahogany table. "Is everything okay? I know I've been…" I rolled my shoulders, not ready to admit to the quagmire of Mitch-drama I'd landed myself in, not even to Calvin. "But you can always talk to me. I'm still here."

Calvin stopped fiddling with placing his scarf just so and gave me a considering look. After a few seconds, a soft smile lightened his expression. "Thank you, that… It means a lot to hear you say that."

Despite the nice way he said it, I felt sucker-punched. What the fuck had I missed? How shitty of a friend did I have to be not to know something was clearly going on with him? I shifted the full weight of the bag to my shoulder and walked with him out of the library. Once outside, I cleared my throat and glanced at him out of the corner of my eye. "So, um, *is* there something you wanted to talk about?"

He turned slightly to look at me and lifted a dark brow as we set off in search of sustenance. "Is there something *you'd* like to talk about?"

I nearly swallowed my tongue. It never ceased to amaze me just how *good* Calvin was at reading people. You'd think after four years of friendship I'd be able to remember these things. But I'd also been a major suck of a friend lately. The least I could do was give him honesty. "Short answer? No. Long answer…yes."

He threw his head back with a hearty laugh. "Those are both short answers, Gallagher."

I chuckled and rubbed the side of my nose. "Suppose they are."

"Maybe. But I think I know what you mean, and I'm right there with you."

I paused on the sidewalk. The savory scents of authentic Italian wafting around us from one of our favorite places. "Really?"

"Yeah." He nodded a few times. "Yeah," he repeated, then gestured to the entrance of Capri. "How about here?"

"Smells good to me."

He laughed and pushed open the door, simultaneously signaling the host for two while holding the door for me. "Seriously, Andy, don't you have enough books?"

"That would be like me asking if you have enough art supplies," I countered as I let the heavy bag drop to the floor and took a seat at the table they had directed us to. Thankfully, we seemed to have beat the dinner crowd and hadn't needed to wait.

"Which you've totally done," he said in an appropriately scandalized voice. Unlike at the library, Calvin removed both his scarf and jacket, which he draped with care over the empty chair beside him before settling in.

I waved him off and kept my sweater decidedly on. It was always too cold in this place. "Know what you're having?" I asked as I peered at the menu.

"Still thinking. You?"

"Leaning toward my usual."

"Of course you are," he mumbled as he continued to peruse his own menu with intense focus, as if we hadn't been here dozens of times.

The server approached the table, effectively heading off my rebuttal. "Good afternoon. My name is Patrick. What can I get you?"

"Two waters to start, and I believe I'm ready to order." I glanced at Calvin, who gave me a quick nod, then passed my menu to Patrick. "I'll have the chicken and shrimp carbonara."

Calvin snapped his menu shut and passed it to the server as well. "And I'll have the day's special."

Patrick tucked the menus beneath an arm. "How would you like your steak?"

"Medium, unless the chef would recommend it another way. Thank you."

Patrick nodded. "Will there be anything else?"

"Fried mozzarella," we said the same time. "And a side of sour cream," I added.

"I'll have your waters right out," Patrick said before leaving to put our order in.

I leaned back in my chair and looked at Calvin. "You had no idea the special today featured steak, did you?"

"*No*," he groaned. "And now I *really* want a bottle of Hamacher Pinot Noir." He gave an exaggerated pout. Besides the fact that I seriously doubted they had that exact bottle here, no way were they serving us alcohol without our IDs showing twenty-one.

"Woe is you," I said with a laugh.

"For real." He glanced off in the direction our server had gone. "Maybe Patrick will be my consolation dessert," he said wistfully.

"Calvin!" I shout whispered and tried not to let my laughter get out of control.

He shrugged. "What? He's cute."

I rolled my eyes and shook my head. "Okay, yeah, he is kind of cute."

Calvin did a prim shoulder shrug as if to say "See?" then he unrolled his cutlery with a flourish, placing the napkin across his lap. "Now I want to hear all about how your application to Chicago is going."

Our waters arrived—mercifully, after we'd both admitted to how cute the server was—and I lifted my glass. "Only if you do the same."

He smiled and mirrored me, clinking our glasses together. "Done." We never really talked about how we might end up at the same university, but I had to confess, the possibility held a certain amount of appeal.

Chapter 19

Mitch

I smiled at Brian's antics as the team filed out of the lockers, a little because I should and a little because I wanted to. We may not see eye to eye on a lot of things, but I couldn't begrudge his dedication to the team or his rightful title of captain. Also, there was the small fact that he was supposed to be my best friend…on the team anyway. The fight in the hall had already become old news, swept under the rug and out of sight exactly like I'd expected it would. Of course, just because no one was talking about it didn't mean I wasn't still paying the consequences.

The team split apart into predetermined groups for drills, and I fell in step beside Hendricks and Smith to run laps around the practice field. The three of us settled into an easy jog to warm up that would undoubtedly turn into grueling sprints the second coach realized his shitlist wasn't giving it their all. I glanced over at Oliver Smith and wondered what he'd done to land himself here. Hendricks, I knew. Guy tried way too hard to stand out. And while he had talent, he played angry, like he had something to prove, and too often let his mouth run away with him. For that alone, he'd probably never make it to a starting a position.

Head down, focus ahead, do as you're told. That's the only way any of us make it out of here.

I followed my advice and hunkered down, pulling ahead of the others. At least today, my ass didn't hurt like it had been when the coach had originally ordered me to run laps before practice. I shook my head and pushed the memory away. Practice would never be a safe place to think about Andy. Not the way he hadn't hesitated to tell me exactly what to do or the way he'd taken care of me, and definitely not the way he'd seemed to genuinely care. I growled to myself and poured on more speed until my lungs and legs burned in unison.

Browning grass raced beneath my feet and in my periphery, I caught sight of the other two gaining ground. We made another complete circuit and Coach glanced our way, but didn't give us the nod to stop. I growled my frustration at being forced to continue instead of training properly like the others. My gaze flicked over at a low laugh beside me, where Connor's long legs easily kept pace with my strides.

"Welcome to the B-team. How many weeks is this now?"

"Fuck off, Hendricks."

He did a bit of fancy footwork that undoubtedly had gotten him on the team in the first place and started running backwards, now doing double time to keep up. "Hey, does this mean you'll be riding the pine this spring and someone else will get to play for change?" He smirked, and I debated telling him it was his smart mouth keeping him from starting.

"We're supposed to be running, not talking." I pushed my straining limbs harder to outstrip him, but the fucker switched to running normal again.

"Yeah, but talking is more fun. Besides, you're not *winded*, are you? Maybe you should volunteer to take a back seat and let someone else shine."

"Chill out, Connor," Oliver wheezed behind us, struggling to keep up with our increasing speed. "Are you trying to dig us in deeper?"

Connor made a dismissive noise. "Relax. It's not like *we're* the ones who've been blowing off practice and showing up late or being half-assed."

I let the digs wash over me. Connor could say whatever he liked; it wouldn't change anything. No matter how much I might wish otherwise, I would keep starting short of a major injury and he would stay second string.

"Hudson!" My head snapped around at Coach S's shout. "Get your ass over here and show Walters and Monroe how to do a proper BTB."

"Yes, Coach," I replied instantly, and peeled away to join the group of demoralized, frustrated faces, even though a stitch already burned along my side and my feet ached from the relentless running. A water break would have been great, but as Coach's hawk eyes tracked me across the field, I thought better of it. I'd take my licks and keep going. I knew what I was getting into the second I'd decided to try to win Andy back, and I refused to have any regrets.

Andy

I closed the paperback and basked in the fleeting euphoria of having finished a good book. The fantastical escapades of a prince from another dimension stealing across the vale to abduct not one, but two brides in order to keep the magic in his kingdom alive had been an unexpected delight, with far more romance than I'd predicted. That hadn't diminished my overall enjoyment of the book though and I eagerly anticipated the sequel due to release next spring. Honestly, the only thing that could have possibly made the story better would have been if the unwitting king had found a groom instead of a bride.

A sigh escaped me as I rested my head against the wall and wondered if Mitch had finished his space pirate book yet. I didn't expect that he had, but I did hope that he'd at least started it.

"Something bothering you?" Lucien asked as I reached for another book inside the dragon tote.

"Just the usual dysphoria of finishing a good book."

Lucien nodded in understanding and returned to emptying his satchel of the notes from his study group. "Series?" he asked over his shoulder.

"Next year."

His face twisted in mock pain. "Harsh."

"Yeah. Interested?" I held up the nearly discarded paperback.

He straightened and held out a hand. "I'll take a look." I tossed it over without a second thought. "Genre?" he asked as he snagged it out of the air.

"Fantasy with a touch of realism."

"Cool." He flipped it over and began perusing the back jacket. A couple of minutes later, he nodded to himself and tucked the book beside his desk lamp. "Is it okay if I get it back to you after the holiday weekend? Normally I'd get it to you sooner, but I'm actually bouncing early."

"No problem at all. Early, huh? Must be nice."

He shrugged and pulled his button down over his head. "Eh, it might not be so bad if they didn't expect me to participate in all the religious shit."

"Family still ignoring you're atheist?"

"Yep." He tugged on a plain tee and switched out his khakis for more comfortable lounge pants, then flopped on the bed in a giant puff of expelled air.

"At least you'll have something good to read to distract yourself."

"Hell fucking yes." He leaned forward to snatch his current book from the desk and settled down.

I chuckled to myself and settled in with my fresh story. Twenty minutes later, I realized I'd yet to move from page three, but couldn't tell if it was the story itself I couldn't seem to get into or that my focus had gone up in smoke. My mind kept straying to an alternative story line for the book I'd just finished, one in which the dashing prince who had no desire to be king fell for a cute lab assistant with red hair and an inquisitive mind. I pushed the fantasy away, but it kept coming back, and each time the prince looked more and more like Mitch.

Damn it, I never should have had sex with him.

A groan drifted out of me, and Lucien shifted on his bed. I refrained from glancing over to see if he was looking at me and doubled down on my efforts to engage with the words perched on my lap. The harder I tried, though, the more the words blurred until I gave up and switched it for a different book from the bag. When I reached down, I caught Lucien gazing over at me curiously. I studiously ignored the look and opened the new book without even glancing at the back jacket or title.

Not even a paragraph in, I'd already slid into a revision of one of the hottest scenes of the reluctant king story. One in which the stubborn prince pressed the unwitting extra bride against the wall in the lab, except it wasn't the sassy maiden, but me whose shoulders pressed into unforgiving iron and wood as Mitch conquered my mouth and wedged his leg between my thighs. The scene didn't even take that much imagination as Mitch had done much the same in the secret room at the start of term. His hot mouth searing kisses into my skin while his fingers dug mercilessly into my sides and forced all my want to the surface.

I jerked violently at the sudden rush of longing that flooded through me and pinched the bridge of my nose to ground myself. The move did shit for all to relieve the stress behind my eyes or quell my rising erection.

"You okay over there?"

I fumbled the book in my hands, nearly tossing the damn thing across the room, and ended with it clutched against my chest like the meager pages would attempt to break free and fly away of their own accord. Upside, my chub was definitely gone now. "Uh, yeah..."

Lucien stared at me for a solid second without blinking, then turned his attention back to his own book. I let out a sigh and tried to do the same. "You, uh, wanna talk about it?" he asked awkwardly.

I chewed on my lip and debated the wisdom of trying to talk to Lucien about my issues, not in the least bit tricky because I couldn't actually say anything about Mitch and I wasn't about to tell him I was gay. "Um... I have this...report," I floundered.

"Okay. What about it?"

"It's...not going the way I expected?"

"Are you asking or saying? What's the report about? A class we share or one on your own?"

I instantly regretted the attempt to seek an unbiased opinion about my predicament at the rapid-fire questions. "That's not important," I said.

Lucien's face scrunched up in a confused scowl and his book tipped back, momentarily forgotten.

"I mean, the issue isn't the report itself so much as I think I'm on the wrong track. If you'd asked me four y-weeks ago," I quickly amended, "I could have told you exactly how I would have finished it, but now... Now I seem to have gone off on a weird tangent and I don't think my original...thesis holds." I risked another glance at Lucien to see what he was making of my awkward as fuck attempts to relate the situation I now found myself in with Mitch.

His mouth twisted to the side as it usually did whenever he was thinking hard. Finally, he said, "If the new thesis isn't working, drop it. Sounds to me like you already know what the report needs. You're just too scared to go for it."

I turned to face forward as Lucien's words sank in. Weird as it sounded, he might be onto something. Except...except pursuing the original thesis meant going back on every promise I'd ever made to myself. Fuck, now I was using this ridiculous metaphor with myself.

"Hey, Anderson?"

I glanced up, but Lucien still had his gaze focused on the book in his lap. "Yeah?"

"If you wanted advice about dating, you could have just said so." His lips quirked up in a half smile and he looked at me out of the corner of his eye.

So much for being cunning.

"Right. Yeah. I'll remember that…next time," I said to fill the void. He gave a small nod and returned his full attention to the book he was pages from completing. I, on the other hand, suffered in silence, running over all the ways the situation with Mitch could blow up in my face at any second, and never made it past the first page.

Chapter 20

Four Years Ago

Andy

Showered and dressed to face the day, I ventured out in search of my best friend. It took an active effort to keep my face from splitting into a grin as I walked the halls. I exited the West Hall and made my way to the Green and the muted hum of cheerful voices. I quickened my pace, practically racing the last several yards, eager anticipation fueling me until at last I vaulted over the low wall that still bore marks of our misguided firework prank.

The smile I'd fought so hard to keep at bay broke free as my gaze fell instantly on Mitch. He stood laughing with some of the other team hopefuls, including his new roommate, Nate. The smart thing to do would be to wait until later to tell him the rest of what I should have told him the night before, but my excitement trumped my patience. I took a few steps closer and raised a hand to catch his attention. When that didn't work, I called out.

"Mitch!"

His gaze swept in my direction, but didn't settle, although no one else was nearby. Then he turned back to Nate and laughed again. My smile dissolved.

He looked right at me. No. He looked right through me, like I wasn't even here, like last night hadn't happened, like…like… He acted like he doesn't even know me.

My breath hitched, and I stumbled backwards. How delusional could I be? There wasn't a snowball's chance in hell Mitch could ever feel the same way about me, no matter what had happened last night. We'd all heard stories about some of the more interesting things that the boys of Ulwich Prep had been caught doing. It didn't mean anything. But it did to me and my best friend would know that, except…except he wasn't looking at me.

I ached to call to him again, demand that he see me, acknowledge what had happened between us, but I couldn't pull in enough air to convince sound to come out of my mouth. Tears pricked my eyes and I shook my head.

This has to be a dream. A really, really bad dream. Mitch couldn't…wouldn't abandon me like this. Not my Mitch.

Yet there he went, across the Green without so much as a half-hearted wave or blink in my direction. As far as he was concerned, I didn't exist. It wasn't until my back bumped into the low stone retaining wall, I realized I hadn't stopped retreating.

"Hey, Gallagher."

I glanced up from my imploding world at the greeting. "Hi, Bridges," I offered and immediately returned my attention to Mitch's receding form, which was currently being swallowed by the rest of the lacrosse team. Why wouldn't he look at me?

"Does he know you're in love with him?" The whispered question right next to my ear practically sent me shooting out of my skin. I spun around to confront Calvin. His characteristically unkempt curls hung in his face as he leaned against the low wall. He swept them out of the way, revealing dark brown eyes set in a lighter brown face dominated with open curiosity.

"What? No. Why would you say that?" I glanced off to the side, illogically terrified that he could have somehow heard something I'd never been brave enough to voice aloud.

Calvin glanced toward the players where they were starting an impromptu match. Then his features clouded with confusion and he shifted his attention back to me, his dark brows scrunched together. "He at least knows you're gay, right?" he asked clearly, though not loud enough to be heard by anyone not right next to us.

My eyes widened at this fresh horror. There wasn't a doubt in my mind that fear was plastered clear as day across my face as I looked back to where Mitch was being congratulated by his new teammates.

New friends.

I brought my gaze back to Calvin, swallowing past the hard lump threatening to cut off all my air. "So, it's true. You really are…" I trailed off, not bold enough to say it aloud as he clearly was. More than a few rumors centered around Calvin's sexuality.

He shrugged and held his hands out. "I am who I am. I'm proud of it and don't see any reason to change just because it makes some people uncomfortable."

I stared, amazed at his level of confidence and a little envious. It had taken me almost fourteen years and an insane attraction to my best friend for me to come to this realization, but he acted as if he'd always known.

He rested his elbows on the wall and stared right back. "I also notice you didn't deny it."

My jaw dropped. However, trepidation quickly overrode the astonishment. How did he know? Did everyone know? Were there rumors about me too? Was that why Mitch didn't want to be seen with me?

Calvin picked up on the shift and held out his hands again, this time in a placating gesture. "Don't worry, your secret is safe with me. If you don't want anyone to know, no one will. Though, full warning, being seen with me might make you guilty by association," he added with a crooked smile.

I let out the breath I was holding and cast one last look at the spot where Mitch had completely ignored my existence. "He knows," I whispered. Calvin's face fell at my tone, as did his hands. My own fisted by my side as a tide of self-loathing rolled through me. "I told him what I am. I… I don't think we're friends anymore."

"Who."

I glanced up sharply. "What?"

"Who," he repeated. "You told him *who* you are. You're not a 'what' Andy, you're still human, just like he is."

I shook my head, unable to accept what he was saying. It certainly didn't feel that way. The rejection stabbing through my heart threatening to rip it in two was testament to that.

"How did it go when you told him?" Calvin asked cautiously, inching a little closer.

I thought back to our unbelievable night, what he'd said, what we'd done. My traitorous heart, still freshly bleeding, fluttered at the memory. "Not at all like I expected." Calvin raised an eyebrow at the unusual response. "It's complicated," I added without elaboration.

His curious expression morphed into an amiable smile. "I like complicated."

Present Day

Andy

I stared down at the book in my hand, already having forgotten why I picked it up. The week had been a special kind of mind fuck and clearly my retreat to the library and the crassness that was Calvin were not proving to be the diversion I desperately needed. I still couldn't believe I'd had sex with Mitch. It was one rule. One. Nevermind that we'd both gone on like nothing had happened, nothing had changed. The only mercy was the fact that Mitch hadn't pointed out that I'd been the one to break it.

"I'm telling you, one of these days he'll realize the error of his ways," Calvin said as he replaced one book only to remove another. I looked up from my tumultuous thoughts and wracked my brain to figure out what we were talking about now. Calvin was notorious for skipping around in a conversation.

I glanced around for some sort of clue. Shelves rose around us, cluttered with books and creating a haven of reclusion from the rest of the library. It wasn't perfect, but it offered a modicum of privacy for some of our more…interesting conversations. At last, my mind caught up with what he'd said and I rolled my eyes.

"I still don't get it. I mean, Benny. Of all the people to have a crush on…" I glanced over at Calvin, curious if he'd deny it.

When he didn't even acknowledge it, I shook my head. "Seriously though, he's such an ass."

"But, you see, that *is* why." He held out his hands for emphasis and stared between them like he really could see Benny's ass. "Mm, you don't even know. Boy's got an ass you could bounce a quarter off of." Despite my own pervasive funk, I couldn't help but laugh at the lascivious look he gave the imaginary ass. Calvin was hands down the lewdest person I'd ever known and while we may not agree on a lot of things, I wouldn't give up his friendship for the world.

The muffled sound of books falling to the carpeted ground snatched the humor from my lungs. I immediately shoved my nose back in my book which turned out to be one of my acquisitions from the book store. The topic of murder seemed appropriate as the source of the disruption sauntered into our cultivated bubble.

"Look at what we have here. It's Club Faggot." The usual three culprits followed the insult. Benny's lackeys laughed at the tired insult while their fearless leader rested a shoulder on the nearest stack and glared at us. He gave no hint that he recalled the threat I'd given him in the hall that day, nor had he ever sought me out.

"Fuck off," I said, doing my best to ignore the vulgar charades Neil and Todd were performing behind him. "We're not bothering anyone."

Benny's face twisted into a sneer. "You're bothering me." The palpable shift in mood made the alcove shrink from small to minuscule. The hair on my arms stood on end and I could practically feel Calvin gearing up for a verbal fencing match.

"Then leave," I suggested in an attempt to prevent things from escalating.

"What if I don't want to? What are you going to do about it?" Benny pushed off of his perch, inspecting his fingernails as he ventured deeper into our sanctuary, then knocked over the stack of books Calvin had been creating. His goons snickered in the background while Calvin made a sound that was a cross between an indignant squawk and an angry growl.

"I'm gonna start by getting Professor Jackson," I said quickly, aiming for nonchalance as I glanced up from my book. "I don't think he'd appreciate learning how you're treating the materials."

"Oh yeah? And how do you think he'd appreciate finding out about you two fucking up here?" Benny snarled back.

Calvin gasped and struck an exaggerated pose of insulted horror. "We are in a sacred space of learning. And, *ew*." He looked at me for emphasis, mouth agape at the preposterous notion.

I rolled my eyes and went back to my reading, determined not to let any of their prodding get to me. I had enough problems to contend with without adding someone else's homophobia to the mix.

Benny sucked on his teeth and took a step back. Bully he may be, but he wasn't stupid. He couldn't prove we'd been doing anything suspect, and forcing the issue would only draw attention to his own involvement. "Whatever, homos." He made one last hideously vulgar gesture and stalked off, closely followed by Todd and Neil.

"One of these days," Calvin commented wistfully as he watched Benny leave.

I glanced after the trio. "I'm not one to judge—really, I'm not—but seriously? How can you still say that? He's a jerk and he'll always *be* a jerk." Calvin's only response was to hold his hands back up and wriggle his eyebrows suggestively. I threw my hands up in defeat. "To each his own."

"Speaking of which, you still carrying that flame for Mitch?" he asked without even glancing over his shoulder.

Some days, I really regretted telling Calvin what had happened four years ago. Not the whole thing, but enough. I groaned. So much for not thinking about it.

"You're friends again, right? You've been spending a lot of time together at the very least," he added, switching books once more from the now rebuilt stack.

"You could say that. And for the record, I'm trying to keep that *particular* light extinguished." *Not that it's working.* I shook my head. "But he makes it really hard. I don't think he has any idea how hard he makes it."

"I *bet* he doesn't." I met Calvin's snide response with a book to the shoulder. "Ow," he said, rubbing the point of impact. "Have you told him?"

"I'm trying to make things better, not worse." I hadn't told him the whole truth four years ago, and I had no intention of doing so now.

"Just saying. Maybe if you slept with him…" I shot Calvin an angry look in lieu of another book. He held up his hands defensively. "It was just a suggestion."

"The whole thing is a mess." I hung my head and massaged my aching temples. There was absolutely no way I was going to tell him I'd tried that, and it hadn't done shit. If anything, I was more confused than ever.

Calvin abandoned his books and sat beside me. "If you would tell me more about what happened that night, maybe I could help better."

I glanced at him from the refuge of my folded arms. "I've been dreaming about it again."

Calvin's face fell. "Judging by the way you say that, it's not the good bits."

I shook my head and buried my face back in the protection of my arms. "It's always the same. I wake up cold and alone. I search the room, but there's no clue to where he went. He's just...gone."

We sat in silence for a minute while I relived the nightmare. The aching cold that had settled into my bones without a warm body beside me to stave off the chill. The naïve joy swallowed by despair when I realized he was never coming back, not to the secret room, not to me, not ever. I stared unseeing over my arms at the sculpture of books Calvin had created. The colors blurred together indiscriminately, and the architecture became a shapeless blob.

"I remember thinking at the time how smart he was to already have gone, that he was protecting us. So we wouldn't get caught together." My chest constricted as I fought back a sob. Four years didn't make the truth of it hurt any less. If anything, recent events made it hurt more.

Calvin's warm hand steadily rubbed along my back, a reassurance that only pushed me closer to falling apart.

"He's going to do it again. He's going to ghost me. I can feel it," I croaked. It wasn't until the words left my mouth that I realized that was the root of my distraction, the unshakable fear that Mitch would get close only to abandon me again.

"Maybe you should do it first."

"We both know I can't do that anymore than you can let go of what happened with Benny."

The back rub suddenly turned into a gripping side hug. "Benny," Calvin said wistfully. He glanced over at me with his characteristic exuberance. "Did I ever tell you about that shower?"

I laughed despite myself and used the palm of my hand to rub away the evidence of my near meltdown. The fear was still there, bubbling beneath the surface, but I welcomed the distraction. "Only like a hundred times."

"There I am, innocently walking into the showers, minding my own business," he went on undeterred. "And who do I find?"

"Benny," I supplied.

"Benny," he echoed. "Jacking off in the shower."

I laughed again at his animated retelling of a story I'd heard enough times to tell myself and had used to bluff Benny into backing down.

"Being the gentleman I am—"

I snorted. Calvin was about as far away as Benny was from being a gentleman.

"Excuse you," Calvin reprimanded me. "Like I was saying. Being the gentleman I am, I coughed to *discreetly* let him know he had an audience."

I couldn't help but wonder how long he'd had the audience before the "discreet cough".

Calvin ignored my snicker and continued his elaborate tale. "In true Benny fashion, he turns to me and says, 'You just gonna stand there, or are you gonna help?'" His mimic of Benny's gruff voice sounded more like a bad noir crime film than a real person.

"What did you do?" I prompted on cue.

"What was I supposed to do? He *literally* invited me. Now, in my defense," he held up a finger for emphasis, "I was only planning on giving him head. How was *I* supposed to know how he was going to want to finish?" His eyes opened wide as if he himself still couldn't believe the unexpected turn of events.

I chuckled. Against all my efforts to remain sullen, Calvin had cheered me up. He had a gift for that, and one I'd cherished since we'd first become friends.

"I still dream about that ass," he sighed, staring off into the distance dreamily.

"You're ridiculous," I said and shoved him in the shoulder. He swatted me away, but thankfully returned to Earth. "One of these days, Benny is going to end you."

Calvin scoffed at the threat as he jumped back up. "Bet you Benny still dreams about it too," he said with a wink.

Mitch

My lunch tray slid across the table, its contents virtually untouched. "But get this," Andy continued his tale, his arms waving animatedly and his eyes sparkling with humor. "Carver then has the audacity to ask if the 1940 version was that different from the 2005."

I leaned across the table, my lunch completely forgotten. "He did not."

"He totally did," Andy said, trying to get his laughter under control enough to continue the story.

"Everyone knows the 1995 mini-series is the best. I mean, Mr. Darcy."

Andy's eyes widened, and he smacked the table. "Right!" We laughed at the same time and he struggled to sober up.

"What did Garza have to say?" I prompted.

"So, I shit you not. Garza looks him dead in the eye and says, '1813'. No one in the room is even breathing at this point. Carver is fucking oblivious and is now insisting that there was no such version and he can't be penalized for something he couldn't find. Garza narrows his eyes—I swear Mitch, I've never seen anyone look so insulted in my life. Anyway, he straight up deadpans, 'The book, not the movie.'"

I smothered a laugh. "Please tell me Carver stopped talking."

Andy leaned back, the light sparking in his green eyes. "God, no. Dumbass then goes on to say, 'Wait, there's a book too?'"

"He didn't," I groaned.

"I thought Garza was going to kill him right there."

"With, what? Laser beam eyes?"

Andy waved a finger at me. "You laugh, but if looks could kill, Carver would be walking around with two holes burned right through his skull."

"How did he even get into your class?"

He shrugged and scooted his tray back in front of him. "Probably used Spark Notes."

I bit my lip to keep from laughing and placed a hand next to his tray. "Wait."

Andy glanced up, his water bottle already to his lips.

"You mean I could have been using those this whole time?"

He snorted water up his nose and spluttered it out all over his neglected tray.

"What? I'm serious."

He reached across the table and shoved me. "Fuck you."

"It was too easy. Also, you know I would never. Lit may not be my forte like it's yours, but I at least respect books enough to read them."

His lips quirked into a smile despite that he was still avidly cursing me. "Fucker, you owe me a new lunch. No, more than lunch, two puddings at the very least."

"You want me to filch you puddings from the kitchen?"

"You heard me."

"You realize I could probably ask for a dozen and they'd hand them over no questions asked?"

His green eyes sparked with mischief. "What's the matter, Mitch? Afraid you've lost your touch? Besides, everyone knows they taste better when they're stolen."

My grin stretched from ear to ear. "And will I have a partner in crime for this little escapade?"

"Do you need one?" he asked, the challenge clear.

"Need is a strong word."

He smirked. "Admitting defeat already?"

"I said, *need* is a strong word… But what if I *want* one?" I clarified, leaning forward once more to rest my arms on the table. "What do you say?"

His eyes darted between mine as he pondered the proposal. I held perfectly still and waited in silence. At last, he stopped chewing on his lip and smiled. "Okay, but we go now."

"Now? Andy, are you nuts? It's the middle of lunch period."

He lowered his voice to a conspiratorial whisper. "What's the matter? Chicken?"

"Never. Bring it. What's the plan?" I asked just as quietly, intending to call him on his bluff. I should have known better. Andy didn't bluff.

He glanced around to make sure no professors or snitches were nearby before hunkering close enough that our foreheads almost touched. My mind flashed to his red lashes fanning across his freckled cheeks as he blinked and looked up at me, eyes filled with doubt, lips parted… Then the memory was gone. "You'll get up first." He pointed subtly, his hand hidden between us, back toward the kitchens. "Carla still has a sweet spot for you, says you look just like her grandson."

"And how do you know that?"

He rolled his eyes. "Because she says it literally every time you go down the line." I couldn't help but smirk at learning that Andy knew that. "Shut up, you're getting off track. Anyway, return your tray straight to her and ask about her grandson. You don't have to get too involved, just enough to keep her distracted while I slip around the line."

"Okay, and how am I supposed to steal the outrageous number of puddings I owe you?"

"Easy. I'm going to create a diversion. Also, two is not exorbitant, and in case you hadn't already guessed, one of them is for you."

"You're so generous," I teased. "Then what?"

"Then we meet back up with our spoils of war."

"The usual spot?" I asked, fully expecting him to know where I was talking about.

He snorted. "Naturally. Ready?"

"Ready." I leaned back, grabbed my tray, and stood like it wasn't weird I was relocating in the middle of lunch.

No one stopped or questioned me as I made my way across the room. I dutifully dumped my trash in the receptacle nearest the line where the lunch custodian Carla was, in fact, conveniently standing. Excitement surged through me as I engaged her in conversation about her grandson Liam, who turned out to also be into lacrosse, while Andy slipped behind her like a flame-haired ghost.

I was just starting to wonder what the distraction was supposed to be and how long I would have to have this pretend conversation when a tower of trays slid free of their perch to clatter loudly on the tiled ground. Carla spun around with a gasp of alarm and ventured into the kitchen to investigate. I followed close on her heels to…help.

She was re-stacking the last of the trays when I slipped away to the massive pantry, still propped open to resupply the line. Andy's determination to go through with the heist made more sense now as I recalled the door had typically been locked when we'd come like thieves in the night to raid its contents. I secured the two puddings as well as some spoons on my way out, then headed straight for the low wall we'd often met at when pranks had been our life.

Andy glanced up when I hopped over the wall and settled down beside him. "What took you so long? I thought you got caught," he said as I tossed him his pudding.

"Me? Never." I held out a spoon for him.

"Please, you totally stayed and helped clean up."

"You say that like you wouldn't have." I bumped his shoulder and his bite of pudding smeared across his cheek.

He let out an indignant yowl and popped my spoon so it splattered chocolate on my nose. "Brown noser," he accused with a laugh, then wiped his face clean.

"Ha ha, you're such a comedian." I searched my bag for a napkin, but had to settle for trying to get it all off with my fingers.

He laughed again and set his pudding aside. "Oh my God, you're hopeless. Come here, before your face turns into Revenge of the

Pudding." He fished out a spare napkin from his bag, wet it with some water from his water bottle, then grabbed my face and turned it towards him. The cool cloth made short work of the mess, but all I could think about was how strong yet gentle his grip was on my jaw. The more I thought about his fingers, the more my face heated, until I was positive I looked like I'd been left to bake for days in a summer sun.

I cleared my throat and pulled away when he finally declared me once again decent for polite society and released me. All of my focus centered on my half-full cup of pudding, but the burn remained. "Any plans for the long weekend coming up?"

"Nah," Andy said, reacquiring his pudding. "Will probably end up staying here and reading since the holidays are coming up. No sense in making the trip back home only to come right back. You?"

"Same. When you say reading, please tell me it's not school books."

He laughed like I hoped he would. "No. I have a new stack I'm working through. Should be able to make some good progress too since Lucien is leaving a few days early."

"No shit."

"Yep." He pulled his last spoonful free and smiled over at me, his green eyes sparkling while the sun set his hair ablaze. "I'll have the whole place to myself starting next Wednesday."

Chapter 21

Andy

I pulled open the door, the scribbled note clutched in my hand. Light pushed into the dusty space of the forgotten classroom from curtainless windows. It had only taken a decade to solidify the nondescript room's reputation as being haunted or, better yet, cursed. When the school had dared reopen it for Professor Marco's exclusive lecture hall five years ago and he'd promptly had a nervous breakdown after a scant three weeks, speculation had burned through every grade like wildfire. Now only the bravest ventured up here and only then on a dare.

"Connor," I whispered as loudly. When no response was forthcoming, I shut the door, mindful of creating any noise that might attract unwanted attention. It clicked shut in almost perfect silence and I turned back to the neglected space. I took a hesitant step forward, my gaze dancing over the desks pushed to the sides, the haphazard cluster of bookshelves shoved together, and the shadows lurking in their depths for any sign of life.

This room isn't really haunted. Pull yourself together.

"Connor?" I called again, louder this time, and immediately felt like an idiot. "That's it, I'm leaving. I don't know why I came up here." I crumbled the familiar scribble, turned to beat a hasty retreat, and came face to face with, well, a face.

"Looking for someone?"

Every hair on my body stood on end and my stomach lurched as my muscles tried to do the same. A jolt of adrenaline sent blood rushing through my ears and made recognition slow in coming. When it did, I could have sprouted claws. "Jesus fucking Christ, Connor. What the hell is wrong with you?"

His uninhibited laughter filled the room, made slightly less creepy now that it held another living being. Though how much longer Connor would remain alive after scaring the living daylights out of me was anyone's guess. He glided his long, lithe frame across the room with the grace of a dancer, completely unperturbed by the fright he'd given me.

"Did you want that alphabetically or by severity?" he asked, his tone light and teasing as he leaned against the monolith of a teacher's desk, his legs stretched out, ankles crossed as he braced on his arms. A broad grin stretched his cheeks and lent a hint of whimsy to his wit. Connor had a special gift to make a joke out of literally anything. Appropriateness need not apply.

I rolled my eyes, my smile threatening to steal across my face. "If you conned me into coming up here just so you could pretend to be a ghost, I'm leaving." *Never should have come up here in the first place. My issues with Mitch are leading me to make even more questionable life choices than usual.* The cruel thoughts wiped away the smidgen of joy Connor's antics had wrung out of me.

In the blink of an eye, Connor vacated his perch and gave up all pretense of his casual repose. "Wait. That's not why." I eyed him skeptically, but didn't venture toward the door. Excitement danced in his eyes as he sidestepped toward the shelves, arms still out to halt my movement. "Besides, if you leave now, you'll miss the best part."

"Best part, huh? And what would that be?" I asked, my repressed smile twitching at the corner of my mouth.

Curiosity killed the cat.

Satisfaction brought it back.

The unwelcome conclusion to the rhyme sounded eerily like Mitch, and it instantly transported my thoughts to when he'd said it to me. With crumbling willpower, I forced the memory away. If I relived it any more, I'd run screaming down the hall. I brought my focus to where Connor had finally made it to the cluster of bookshelves. Guilt coiled like a viper in my stomach as I took in his enthusiastic grin. Connor deserved better. I just couldn't get him to see that.

"Wait right there," he emphasized, before ducking between the shelves. A moment later, his head popped back out, his hair noticeably mussed. "Promise you won't leave."

I rolled my eyes again, making sure he saw the exaggeration. "I promise I won't leave until I see whatever inane surprise you've concocted this time." He flashed another broad grin that nearly split his face in two and vanished again. I moved over to assume his vacated position on the desk. Connor loved surprises...and fun. That's what drew me to him originally. He knew how to have unapologetic fun and I...desperately needed that.

But even good things have their problems.

I stared solemnly down at my feet, lost in my dreary thoughts. Connor wasn't entirely to blame for why we'd broken up. He wasn't even mostly to blame—though I'd let him believe he was. It wasn't my proudest moment, and that guilt was unquestionably what had brought me up here at the whim of a note slipped into my bag, even though I knew this to be a mistake.

The pure note of a trumpet jerked my head up. The instrument was swiftly joined by what had to be a trombone and the more identifiable melody of a piano and bass. A long leg, bare but for a navy sock, emerged from behind the shelves, curling in time with the music. A laugh stuck in my throat as an elaborate arm toss joined the appendage. Connor's long limbs were definitely one of his greatest assets, and he knew exactly what to do with them. He peeked a head out, still not giving away the main event. I shook my head and gave up on restraining my laugh when he waggled his eyebrows at me.

Oh god, please let him be wearing clothes.

The music dipped, and all three revealed pieces retreated. When the brass blared in triumph, he slid out from the curtain right on cue, his socked feet carrying him an extra yard before he came to a complete stop. A loud burst of laughter erupted out of me and I clamped a hand over my mouth, darting an anxious glance over at the door. Connor sashayed his way closer, twirling a monstrous pink boa in time with the salacious music and taking his time crossing the room.

Each swell of music brought a new provocative move. He spun around and glanced over his shoulder at me before shaking his ass like there was no chance of someone happening upon this outrageous show. I sunk my teeth into my bottom lip to hold the laughter at bay. It was for naught. A loud burst of laughter erupted out of me as he trailed the stretch of feather up his body and tossed his head back like it was the most sensuous sensation he'd ever experienced. When he was close enough, he looped the boa over my head and used it to pull himself closer. I struggled once again to muffle my humor. He fake pouted and tossed his head like he was tossing a mane.

"Darlin' you have got to learn to loosen up. Live a little, sweetheart," he drawled despite not being the least bit southern.

I blew a feather out of my face and couldn't help but smile. Getting me to loosen up had become a mission of sorts for Connor. Shame it hadn't taken. "You really are too much sometimes, you know that?" I hooked a finger in his boxers and popped the elastic. The striped light blue cotton and his white undershirt were the only things left of his uniform. Where the hell he'd found the black suspenders, I wasn't sure I wanted to know.

He flipped the boa back around and draped it around himself like a classic lounge singer. "I happen to think I'm just the right amount."

"Perhaps you are," I conceded, now officially grinning.

"There ya go, sugar." He dropped the feathered death trap to hang loosely around his hips and stepped back in close. Habit had my eyes already half-lidded in anticipation. His mouth swiped against mine in a teasing invitation I couldn't help but accept. He draped his long arms around my neck and preceded to explore my mouth with eager abandon. "Missed you," he whispered playfully, angling his hips to show me just how much he'd missed me. If there was one word in the entire English language to describe Connor Hendricks, it would be forward.

I laughed and sought out his defined hip bones beneath the ostentatious feathers. "Connor."

"Connie," he corrected, his voice thick with lust, then recaptured my mouth. His hand glided up my thigh toward my crotch and I lurched back. Suddenly, the saxophone harmonizing with a piano in the background became a discordant jumble of noise instead of the seductive lure it was meant to be.

"No," I said as firmly as I could, considering my tongue had just been in his mouth.

He recoiled at my vehemence. "Is it the name thing? Fuck, Andy, it's not like I even like it all the time." Despite the angry statement, I could still detect the hurt laced underneath.

"Connor—Connie… Fuck." I scrubbed my hands over my face, at a loss for the right thing to say while he continued to put distance between us. How did I let myself keep getting sucked into these situations? Getting back together, even fooling around, would be an epic mistake. "No, that's not it. You *know* that. How many times do I have to tell you?"

His eyes flashed angrily. "Then what?"

"I can't give you what you need. I wish I could." I held my hands out by my sides in a hopeless gesture of surrender.

"Do you?" The sharp words cut me to the quick and guilt welled up.

"I'm sorry." Connor identifying as genderfluid had been an…interesting development in our relationship. I cherished the trust he'd placed in me when he confided how he felt. Given how deeply I cared for him, accepting and supporting him unequivocally had been a foregone conclusion. But that had never been enough to dispel his insecurity. No amount of reassurance would ever convince him that his identity wasn't why we'd broken up. That I wasn't rejecting who he was.

He crossed his arms and tossed his head. "Whatever."

"Don't be like that," I said as I watched the pure vibrancy that was Connor's truest-self disappear beneath a veneer of propriety, projecting what the world expected. His colors dimmed and darkness wrapped around him tighter than the boa. It killed me. "You deserve to be happy."

"So do you, but you won't take your head out of your ass long enough to see that other people are there."

"What is that supposed to mean?"

He tossed aside the boa like it was trash and refused to look at me. In a few steps, he was close enough to the shelves to snag his hidden pants.

"Connie," I said with more force as he began tugging them on.

"Connor," he snapped harsh enough to make me flinch. "I'm weird and queer, Andy, not stupid. Whoever broke your heart did one hell of a job."

I recoiled at the astute accusation. A defense sat unsaid on my tongue. Four years ago, I'd promised I wouldn't tell anyone what had transpired between me and Mitch, and I wasn't about to break that now. Literally the only person who knew had guessed, and I'd been too raw to deny it properly.

Connor let out a heavy sigh and dragged a hand through his unkempt hair. A second of tense silence passed, and he looked back at me, his trousers hanging open at his waist, undershirt half-tucked. "You should go."

"Connor," I said softly and stepped toward him.

He averted his gaze. "Just fucking go, Andy."

I swallowed past the hard lump of guilt lodged in my throat. Without another word, I made my way to the door and slipped silently back into the hall.

Mitch

I shrugged into my jacket and followed the guys out of the West Dormitories. Walking to town to spend an evening staring at half-dressed chicks from the girl's school wasn't exactly my idea of a great time, but showing up didn't just mean for practice. There was a whole song and dance that went with being on the team. You either learned to hum along or suffered the consequences.

Nate nudged my shoulder, his hands already wrist deep in his letterman, and tilted his chin at me. "You sure you're cool with coming along? No one would blame you if you wanted to sit out seeing Ronald and Trixie pawing at each other all night."

Despite his reassurance, I knew no excuse would get me out of this. "Nah, it's fine. Like I said before, I'm cool. She's free to date whoever she wants." So long as it wasn't me.

Brian glanced back at us and slowed his steps until he was close enough to sling an arm around my shoulders. I forced my own to remain relaxed and kept walking like his determination to keep me in check wasn't in any way out of the normal. "Sup, bro?"

"Nothing. Tired from all those damn laps."

"Coach will let up eventually, you'll see," Nate said in support.

Brian squeezed my shoulders, and I bit back a snarl. He was taking this team captain business way too seriously for my liking. "Give him time. Old fucker will forget he's mad." Unlikely, especially when he had so many spies on the team keeping tabs on me. But if I had to run an extra lap for every hour I spent in Andy's company, I'd run a million and never begrudge them.

"Sure," I responded by rote.

"That's the spirit. So you cruzin' for a new honey now that Ronald stole your girl?" Brian teased.

I bit my tongue from reminding him that Trixie wasn't my girl and hadn't been for a while. "Think I'm gonna fly it solo next term." Several pairs of eyes swiveled to stare at me in disbelief. "Keep my head in the game, you know?" I added quickly.

"What about the Finals ritual?" John asked, looking like I'd just told him his grandma had died. Even Nate side-eyed me, and there was nothing pleasant about the look Brian was sending my way. The guys took the whole getting laid before a big game to a new level. It had actually been how I'd lost my virginity… I did not have pleasant memories about the experience. Being tossed into a room by a bunch of rowdy upper classmen and expected to perform with some girl I'd never even met before had been a weight of pressure that made it damn near impossible to do so.

I couldn't help but wonder if my father had been subjected to such ruthless demands or had perpetuated them. I shivered and hoped that wasn't the case. When I'd wanted to join the lacrosse team four years ago, it had been to feel a kind of kinship with a man I could never spend time with again. Sadly, that wasn't what had happened.

"It'll be fine. Don't want to risk getting distracted, especially with all the scouts Coach is planning on bringing." I checked my relieved breath as Brian nodded in acceptance of my answer and released me to stumble along with the others. In his absence, Nate sidled up next to me. I glanced over at him and the telltale line of concern between his brows. "What?"

"You're seriously not going to do it?" he whispered, his gaze darting to the others.

"It's not a big deal, Nate."

"Maybe, but…"

"Look, I have bigger shit on my plate right now than worrying about getting my dick wet in some laxtitute," I snapped.

He held his hands up defensively. "Shit man. I didn't mean any offense. Just wondering is all."

"Leave him be," Brian called from the front of the group. "There's still plenty of time for a pretty little thing to change our boy's mind. Isn't that right, guys?"

I groaned to myself as the heckles of the others circled around me. Just fucking great. Now every last one of them was gonna try to hook me up just so they could keep to their ridiculous superstition of getting laid the night before a major game in order to secure victory.

Chapter 22

Mitch

I padded down the hallway, quiet but confident, no more than another fleeting shadow. Beyond the windows, darkness reigned, punctuated only by a half moon hanging low in the sky. I paused at the junction of passages and checked to make sure the way was clear before venturing into the East Dormitory. It may have been years since I'd taken this journey, but the way was branded into my memory and, at its end, a flame of red that shone like a beacon in my mind's eye.

My foot scuffed on the ground and a sharp squeak rang out into the muffled darkness, gone almost as soon as it emerged. I slunk closer to the wall and looked around. Price was doing the rounds tonight and he could be an absolute ass about violating lights out. Not that I was overly concerned about getting caught. I could sneak out of the entire school and back in with none the wiser…and had. No, it wasn't me I worried about. Then again, it rarely was.

I let out a sigh of relief as my destination came into sight. Once more, I checked to make sure the hall was void of witnesses before crossing it and twisting the doorknob. Pride at my success, however, evaporated when I softly shut the door and found the room completely empty.

Fuck. Where is he?

Lucien, I expected to be gone, but Andy wasn't one for sneaking about unless he had a reason. My stomach soured at what reason my best friend might have to be out of his room at night. The same one that had kept me out of mine perhaps? I ventured over to the desk by his bed and found his latest book lying open to a page, face down, a bookmark beside it. Without thinking, I picked it up and placed the ribbon between the folds of paper and set it back down. Andy hated having bends in the spines of his books.

He wouldn't have left it like that if he didn't intend to return soon.

My gaze caught on the flashlight poking out from behind some of his larger school books, and I smiled. Still a rebellious imp. Andy never could walk away from a good book, usually to the detriment of all else. Which begged the question, what had taken him away now? The obvious answer to all of it was that he'd ducked off to the restroom, Benjamin Price be damned. Reassured in my conclusion, I shifted to a perch where I could easily watch the door without being seen by anyone that might pass in the hallway and resigned myself to wait.

Within a few brief minutes, the knob twisted once more, and the door opened and shut with the barest of clicks. Even with his back to me and the room shrouded in shadow, I'd recognize Andy anywhere. He stood a moment, his hand pressed to the door, then let out a sigh that slumped his shoulders and turned around. The second his gaze landed on me leaning on his roommate's desk, he jumped.

"What are you doing here?"

I frowned and straightened up. "What do you mean? You said—"

My heart fell as Andy's face lit with understanding. Somehow, watching him put together the pieces of my own misguided conclusion was infinitely worse than his surprise.

I'm such a total idiot. I shouldn't have come.

"You're here because I said Lucien went home for the holiday," he stated evenly, then paused and glanced at the floor as if he was searching for something.

Probably a way out of this mess. What was I thinking?

"I can go if you don't want me here," I said, already stepping towards the door. It had been a mistake to come, to believe he wanted me.

Andy's head shot back up and he snared me with those bright green eyes. "What? No. I mean, I suppose I did sort of invite you. Why else would I have told you Lucien had left early?" Hearing the logic out loud didn't make me feel any better. It had obviously been a mistake, and he'd never had any intention of me sneaking in here.

"It's fine," I said, trying to hide my epic disappointment.

"You don't have to go," Andy whispered into the gloom. Saying I didn't have to go was not the same thing as wanting me to stay, and in the darkness, it was nearly impossible to tell which way he was leaning.

With a frustrated sigh aimed more at myself than him, I spun to the window and grabbed the curtain.

"Mitch, wait."

I looked down to see his hand on my arm. Andy appeared equally surprised to find it there, but didn't remove it. I brought my gaze back up to his as the curtains whisked softly behind me. The ambient light pouring through was more than enough to see the slight panic on his face. My hand fell back to my side as I released the thick fabric. "It's okay, Andy."

His hand tightened on my arm and tugged at my pulse. "You can stay."

I searched his face and found no more clarity in the low light than I had in the darkness. "I'll only stay if you want me to." *I won't make the same mistakes again.* When he failed to respond, I had my answer. Some mistakes just couldn't be undone. Wherever the last few months had brought us, we weren't there and probably never would be. "I'll go."

His Adam's apple bobbed in the moonlight and he flicked an anxious glance at the empty bed of his roommate. When his gaze met mine again, he was sporting a small smile that looked a tad forced. "And waste such an incredible opportunity? Besides, you're already here." The hand on my arm relaxed, as did his smile into something more natural, something more Andy.

He still hadn't been exactly clear about *wanting* me to stay, but he was also making it increasingly difficult to leave. Saying no to Andy was never something I'd quite mastered and wasn't sure I really wanted to. I took a step towards him and slid my hand along his cheek to cup his face, then brought my lips to his. He let out a sigh as he melted into the touch, the reaction equally less and more than what he'd given me the last time we'd been truly alone. It was just going to have to do. I used the caress to pull him closer and deepen the kiss. His hand glided along my arm, but didn't go further. I hated how I never felt like I understood the rules with him. They always seemed to be changing, and I always seemed to be losing.

I was about to break free and just call it a night when suddenly, his demeanor shifted. His grip on my arm tightened once more, and the kiss became more aggressive, his tongue sweeping boldly inside my mouth to tangle with mine. The heat of it blindsided me and I reached out with my free hand to grab his waist and steady myself.

As abruptly as he'd deepened the kiss, he released it altogether and stepped back and out of my reach. My hands fells away as he put first one foot, then four between us. An ache I was becoming very familiar with pulsed out to encompass my chest with each pained beat of my heart. I watched in silence as Andy stepped back to the desk by his bed and opened a drawer.

"Plus, the things here are better than what's in a forgotten shack in the middle of the woods," he said, removing a bottle and placing it on top of the book he'd clearly forgotten all about.

The wicked look in his eye and the crooked smile did the rest. I took two long strides towards him and crushed his body against mine. This time, when I kissed him, his hesitation was gone.

Andy

Every fiber of my being ached for Mitch to keep touching me, kissing me, wanting me, and no amount of logic could dispel it. I fisted a hand in the front of his shirt, needing him closer, but still terrified of the cusp I hovered over. This wouldn't be like last time or even the time before that. We weren't fourteen anymore.

It's not too late. I can still stop this.

Our lips danced a hair's breadth apart. However, he didn't take control of the non-kiss. But I wanted him to, I wanted him to take me because I was his, always had been, always would be. Still, he waited in silence for permission.

Always such a gentleman.

I tightened my fingers in the thin fabric of his nightshirt and yanked him closer. Our mouths collided with all the force of years of pent-up frustration, at least for me anyway. While our tongues tangled, his fingers slipped beneath the hem of my shirt where their tips burned molten pools on my side. He kissed me harder and stroked his large hands over my ribs. I moaned into him and the part of my brain responsible for rational thought short-circuited. I needed Mitch with a fierceness I'd never admit to in broad daylight, but here in this bubble of sub-reality, here, I could want.

Maybe…maybe if he has me again, then I can finally move on, let him go.

The wrongness of the whole thing still troubled me. It wasn't right that I suddenly wanted to bottom again, and for Mitch no less, especially since I hadn't been able to give Connor the same. The one and only time we'd tried to switch things up, I'd had an acute panic attack, complete with hyperventilating and body wracking sobs. It had taken Connor hours to calm me down and we hadn't tried again. Undoubtedly, that had contributed to our inevitable breakup along with so many other things. But I didn't want to think about how horribly I'd wronged Connor or how this was probably a terrible mistake. I just wanted to be Mitch's one more time.

All I have to do is stay in control. Remember what this is.

Plan in hand, I relinquished his shirt in order to yank mine off. He quickly followed suit, and I sucked in a breath at seeing his chest laid bare. The light in the shack was inadequate at best, nowhere near enough to appreciate the fine coat of hair dusting his pecks, or the cut of his abs, or the defined V disappearing into his lounge pants. It wasn't until he took a half-step closer that I realized I'd reached out or that I was shaking.

Fuck, pull it together. Stay in control.

And yet, my breath still hitched as my fingers contacted with his chest and splayed out so that my entire palm was pressing against him. Pure want burned through me like wildfire and in the ashes all that was left was need. My gaze flicked up to his. While I couldn't make out the hazel of his eyes, it didn't change the fact that he was watching me in silence. I dragged in a ragged breath as I suddenly realized that I'd stopped breathing the moment I'd touched him.

Control. Stay. In. Control.

I coasted my hand up to cup the side of his neck and pulled him down for another kiss. He leaned into it, owning my mouth while his larger frame crowded me against the bed. I moaned and tangled my fingers in his short hair. Need pulsed in time with my already aching cock. It wasn't enough, it would never be enough.

Fuck it.

I ripped my mouth away from where I was basically trying to eat him and turned around before he could see the flash of desperation on my face. His hands slipped along my waist as he nibbled along the back of my neck, his nose tickling my hair, his moist breath sending shivers down my spine. I pressed back against him and had to smother a whimper at the feel of his cock pressing into my ass. At this rate, he wouldn't even get inside before I came like some pubescent twit first discovering his dick. I flailed blindly around on the desk until my fingers found the bottle of lube.

"Here." The word came out husky and raw, giving voice to all the desires threatening to strip me bare.

He pulled away slightly and took the bottle from me. Anxiety threaded through my delirious need as I moved to remove the rest of my pajamas. His hand closed over my wrist, halting me, and my heart lurched into my throat. "What are you doing?"

"Should think it's obvious." The comment came out snappier than necessary as I fought not to let my fear get the best of me.

He used his hold on me to spin me around. "You sure?" The quiet question ghosted out to stroke my cheek, then slithered its way down to settle in my heart. He was going to make me say it. In that moment, I loved and hated him. I didn't want to admit how much I wanted this, how I burned for him, had never stopped burning. But he didn't deserve to know that. He'd forfeited that right when he'd abandoned me to navigate all of this on my own.

I hovered between indecision and the absolute certainty that I'd already decided about what would happen tonight the second I'd mentioned Lucien leaving early for the holidays. "I'm sure."

Mitch's mouth closed back over mine, gentle and firm, and solidly on the wrong side of all the walls I'd erected around my heart. I wrapped my arms around his neck and arched into him, urging him deeper. He slid a hand down my backside and hooked it under my leg, then with hardly any effort at all, he hoisted me onto the bed. The mattress sank beneath me, much more inviting than an unforgiving floor. I reached greedily for him while at the same time trying to tug my pants off once more.

He joined me on the bed, miraculously free of his own garments, and pressed me into the pillow with another kiss that stole my breath and made my toes curl. I gave up trying to get my pants off and once more wrapped my arms around him, my trimmed nails digging into his back. He shifted to lay a trail of hot kisses along my neck while his hands divested me of my pajamas. I bowed off the bed as his slick fingers wrapped around my dick and stroked. The moan that fell out of me bounced around the room and only made me harder. I struggled to regain control of the situation, but I couldn't see straight, let alone think straight. His fingers danced over my sensitive shaft, then turned their attention to my balls. I writhed beneath the gentle torture.

"For fuck's sake," I hissed, at the end of my rope and hanging on by a thumbnail. "You need to…need to…"

Before I could get the words out, his fingers ventured lower and tapped at my entrance. I gasped as electricity blasted through my system. My entire body tightened, refusing admittance even though this was something I desperately wanted. He leaned forward once more and tangled our tongues in a slow dance that both grounded me and sent me soaring while he continued to rub circles around the sensitive muscle. When his finger slid inside with almost no resistance, I moaned into him. Within a matter of minutes, those moans turned to heavy pants and even louder groans. Then he massaged my prostate and stars danced behind my eyes. Mitch may not have been the smartest kid in school, but he was a fucking incredible student.

I gripped the base of my cock, not ready to let go, and on the verge of begging. Like the astute observer he was, Mitch removed his fingers and replaced them with the head of his swollen cock. He added more lube, then worked his way inside. Every inch, every centimeter threatened to unravel me, until at last he was all the way in, filling me up and making me his. His forehead pressed to mine as we both adjusted to the overwhelming sensation. Then he stole a sweet kiss that made my heart flutter. My fingers dug into his back once more as I fought off the tide of emotion determined to pull me under. Thankfully, he took the response as encouragement and moved, first slowly, then with stronger thrusts until the bed creaked and the sound of our harsh breathing filled the room, punctuated by the occasional moan.

My orgasm danced closer and closer. I drew a shuddering breath and a distant sound tickled my senses. More than lost in the moment, I pushed it away until I realized it was getting louder. My eyes flew open. "Oh, shit."

Mitch paused, concern clear on his face in the moonlight streaming through the window. "What?"

I strained to hear the one sound that could ruin everything. Footfalls. Approaching fast. "Benny. He's coming."

"Fuck. What do—" Mitch didn't have a chance to finish as I pushed him off the bed. He fell with a loud thump and I winced, but there wasn't time for apologies as the doorknob turned.

I quickly lay back down and wrapped a hand around my flagging cock. The ensuing moans were purely theatrical and the best I could do given the circumstance. I didn't dare look down to see if Mitch had scooped his clothes under the bed with him. My hand continued to stroke my cock with a fervor that sparked a bit of life. The door opened and I willed myself to keep going.

"What the fuck is going on in here?" Benny asked, his gaze sweeping the room for something—or someone—that shouldn't have been there. When his gaze landed on me, his face twisted in revulsion. "Fucking hell, Gallagher."

Not an exhibitionist by any stretch, it took everything I had to keep moving. "Ever heard of knocking?"

"Jesus, you fucking fag. Stop."

"Since when is it a crime to get off?"

"I'm right here," he snapped, a scowl stamped across his face.

I raised an eyebrow and deliberately stroked up slowly, adding a moan for good measure. "Are you just going to stand there, or are you going to help?" The look of furious outrage that exploded across his face was almost worth nearly getting caught with Mitch in my bed.

"Fucking queer, keep that shit to yourself."

"That a no?"

"Go fuck yourself."

"Trying," I fired back without mercy. "So help or get out. What'll it be?"

Rage sprinted across his face, and his cheek twitched. "Keep it down," he ordered, and slammed the door shut. I counted to five and listened for his receding steps before letting out a sigh of relief.

"That was really fucking close," Mitch said as he rose from his hiding place.

"Yeah, it was," I responded and grabbed his arm to tug him back onto the bed. Already my body was perking back up at his proximity.

"Maybe I should go."

I faltered. "You're not done, are you?" I glanced from him to his still erect cock. He ducked his head and I couldn't help but wonder if he was blushing.

"Did you finish? Sounded like it got pretty close."

Ooh, Mitch liked to listen. That was interesting. I shook my head and reached for him again. My fingers scratched along his scalp as our lips came together once more.

"Are you sure?" Mitch asked. I nodded and got as far as my tongue in his mouth before he threw the brakes again. "Aren't you worried he'll come back?"

I let out a frustrated huff and refused to give up my hold on him, not now that I finally had him in my grasp. "Trust me, Benny won't come back here tonight for anything short of an explosion. Now are you good? Because I'm gonna need you to finish what you started." Without waiting for a response, I slammed our mouths back together.

Mitch's capable fingers ventured once more to my ass and I let out a deep groan as he sought out my prostate. Between heart beats, his hard length replaced his fingers. Every nerve sparked back to life as I clung to him and continued to conquer his mouth as he conquered my body. Kissing became more difficult as each thrust stole more of my breath. He cradled my back with one hand and moved his other to cup my ass. The firm hold pulled me further open, and he slid a fraction deeper.

"Mitch," I gasped, his name falling like a whispered prayer from my lips as I fell back.

He followed after, sucking fervent kisses on my neck and anywhere else he could reach before at last wrapping a hand around my aching cock and stroking in time with his increasingly rapid thrusts. I wrapped my legs around him, altering the angle just enough so that the next few thrusts stroked my prostate just right. My breath caught, and I clawed at his shoulders, needing to hang onto something as he systematically took me apart.

"Come for me." His growl went through me like an arrow.

I grunted as the pain of it shattered me into a million pieces. The shock of my climax was still rolling through me when he jerked above me. His release spilled inside, filling me with a warmth that would have made me come if I hadn't already.

He leaned down to swipe my lips with a kiss once more before collapsing to the side. "Fuck."

Yep. That about summed it up. The instant the post bliss haze cleared, logic rushed in to fill me with cold. *What have I done? What part of that was staying in control? Fuck fuck fuck.*

I slipped off of the bed and thanked my lucky stars my knees didn't buckle; they were certainly shaky enough, not to mention the characteristic sting in my ass all but guaranteed that I wouldn't be doing anything comfortably for the next day or so. Oddly enough, I didn't give a shit.

Worth it.

I pushed the echo of the thought from four years ago away and pulled out a mostly clean shirt from the hamper. It wasn't perfect, but it would do. I cleaned up the best I could and glanced out of the corner of my eye to see Mitch doing the same. Deafening silence filled the room and while I ached to fill it, I couldn't find the words that wouldn't ruin what we'd just done. I bent to grab my pajamas from the floor and did a double take at seeing Mitch climbing back into the bed. The plaid fell from my suddenly numb fingers.

"What are you doing?"

"I'm gonna need a minute," he said as he flopped back and made himself comfortable.

The urge to argue the impracticality of him lingering even a second longer than necessary rose and promptly died. After all, hadn't I been the one to say that Benny wouldn't bother us for anything short of nuclear fallout? And it wasn't exactly like I was eager for Mitch to go.

So much for self-preservation and controlling the situation.

I grumbled to myself about my total inability to deny him and crawled in beside him on the narrow bed. "Fine," I conceded, spearing him with a glare, "but only for a minute. And don't you dare fall asleep."

"Yeah, yeah. No sleeping, got it. Now scoot over."

"Me? You're the one taking up all the room, you damn giant. Why don't you go lay on Lucien's bed, then you'd have plenty of room," I huffed and turned on my side, facing the window and putting my back to him.

"That requires movement. Besides, I'm already here. Now seriously, you're hogging the pillow."

"Ugh." I sat up and punched the pillow back to give him more of it. "It's not my fault you're too big."

"I wasn't too big a minute ago."

My jaw mentally dropped. Looking down at him in the low light, it was nearly impossible to tell if he'd meant for that to be a dick joke. Rather than call him out, I dismissed it and rolled once more to face out as far as the tiny bed would allow. "You're incorrigible," I grumbled.

"You know I don't know what that means."

"Liar."

He chuckled behind me and shifted to commandeer what was apparently his part of the pillow. "Fine, I do."

I barely suppressed a shiver as the warm words caressed the back of my neck. His moving around had brought him substantially closer than I expected, though why this closeness affected me so much when he'd been closer earlier boggled the mind. Suddenly, his long arm draped over my side and his hand felt around the edge of the bed.

"What are you doing now?" I whispered.

"Just making sure you're not gonna fall off."

"I'm fine." Despite my reassurance, his arm stayed draped across me. I hated how much I liked having it there, knowing that although I'd literally thrown him to the floor earlier, he didn't want the same to happen to me. "I mean it, Mitch, don't fall asleep. I don't know how you sneaked in here to begin with, but it will be damn near impossible to sneak out come morning." Silence filled the room like a living thing. I waited a moment, but no response was forthcoming. "Did you hear me?" I pressed.

"I heard you," he whispered. Another tense moment passed and all the anxiety I'd kept at bay snuck out from the depths to plague me once more.

I must be out of my mind. Why did I think this was a good idea? It was one rule…

"Andy?" Mitch's sudden whisper startled me. At my tiny jump, his arm curled around me, pulling me closer.

I swallowed before answering. "Yeah?"

"Why did you let Benny talk to you like that?"

"What do you mean?"

"The gay slurs. Why didn't you stick up for yourself?"

I shrugged, which had the added consequence of Mitch's arm tightening even more. My back pressed firmly against his chest and my heart stuttered. I snuffed the ember that stubbornly refused to stay dead and focused on the unusual query. "There's no point in it. That's just who he is. Benny is harmless. Besides, arguing wouldn't have been conducive to getting him to leave." I expected that to be the end of it, when I felt Mitch's nose brush my hair as he buried his face in the back of my neck. My breath caught and I willed my stupid heart to find a steady rhythm.

"No one is harmless," he whispered, his breath tickling the sensitive hairs. His arm tightened briefly in conjunction with the morose words, at once protective and possessive. I swallowed past the sudden lump lodged in my throat and found no words.

Chapter 23

Four Years Ago

Mitch

A shout came from the opposite end of the makeshift field. I knew I needed to pay attention or risk getting hit by either the ball or a body, but my mind was still stuck on the image of Andy standing on the hill waving emphatically to get my attention. His red hair shone copper in the morning sun and even from this distance, I could see the green of his eyes. My gaze passed right over him and he staggered back as if physically struck. I winced at the echo of the blow that landed in my gut.

What have I done?

Someone tugged on my arm, pulling me back into the game. Sweat trickled down my back as I moved forward to cut toward the goal. I dodged Benny before he could body check me for my trouble and passed the ball to Brian. He was less fortunate evading the Middies. The friendly match continued, but my movements were mechanical, my body moving by rote rather than desire to win.

Eventually, the game came to a stopping point when the existing lacrosse team spilled out onto the Green. Shouts went up as the coach started listing the names of those that had made the cut. I knew I made the team long before my name was called. I knew because Andy had told me so. Against my better judgment, I glanced over to where I'd spotted him earlier. The low stone wall stood immovable at his back, a witness to countless schemes and animated conversations. It was a place I treasured and one that had always brought me comfort. Andy stood staring down at the chaos on the field, except he wasn't alone.

The Senior Captain slapped me on the back and congratulated me again on making the team. His voice joined the rest of the enthusiastic commendations and celebratory cheers. But it was all white noise. All I could see was Andy talking to Calvin Bridges. And Calvin was smiling.

I turned away from the sight twisting my stomach into knots and melded into the crowd. Andy didn't need me. He'd moved on.

It's for the best.

The thought brought me little comfort as the tiny spark of hope that I could somehow be redeemed went out.

Present Day

Mitch

The tension in Andy's body slowly relaxed as his breathing deepened into the steady rise and fall of slumber. I tightened my arm around his waist and pulled him closer into the cocoon of my body, though he was in no danger of falling off. He shifted in his sleep and I feared I'd inadvertently woken him up. But rather than turn and berate me for still being there, he snuggled back against me. I let out a relieved breath and burrowed my face once more against his neck.

He had a point. Sneaking out of a secret room was one thing, sneaking out of a dorm room that wasn't yours was substantially more conspicuous. Despite the logic and the risks, though, I wouldn't leave. Even if he woke right now and demanded I go, I'd stay. I wasn't about to make the same mistake twice.

Not for the first time, more like the millionth, I wondered what would have happened if I had stayed that fateful night. Would Andy have forgiven me? Would he have understood? What if I hadn't turned my back on him the next day or all the days after that? I thought back to the one and only time we'd run into each other before he'd found me on the verge of committing another grave mistake in the Tower at the start of term.

It hadn't even been a year since we'd spoken. He'd come tearing down the hall like hell itself was after him. Too preoccupied with looking over his shoulder, he hadn't seen me crossing from an adjoining hallway. We'd collided. While I kept my footing, he'd gone sprawling. Books tumbled out of his bag, equal parts worn paperbacks and massive texts. He immediately started gathering them and only when the last one was secure did he look up.

The look of abject horror as the blood drained from his face when he realized who he'd run into would haunt me until the day I died. At the steady beat of feet hitting the ground, we both looked back the way he'd come. He turned back to me, the tiniest spark of hope in his eyes when I didn't call attention to where he was. The footsteps got louder and my gaze flicked up to make sure no one had emerged at the end of the hall yet. When I glanced back down at him, he didn't even seem to breathe as he awaited judgment.

"Go." One word. It was all I could manage, and it nearly killed me. He scurried to loop his bag over his head and got to his feet. He took two steps, then hesitated, glancing over his shoulder at me. I wanted to scream at him to run, but more than that, I wanted to run with him, away from this awful place and all the horrible mistakes I'd made. Instead, I turned to face the oncoming threat. I sensed him leave, taking that herbal scent that was wholly his with him.

John, Todd, and Aaron skidded to a halt before me, their gazes searching the otherwise empty hallway. "Oy, did you see where that ginger freak went?"

My jaw tightened, and I forced it to relax. "What's it to you?"

Three pairs of eyes snapped to me. "That queer has it coming," John said, joined by a host of cruel laughter.

It had taken everything in me to keep my shoulders from tightening up. I shoved my hands in my pockets and met his gaze without blinking. "How do you know he's queer?"

"He just is."

I shrugged. "But how do you know?" John frowned and looked to the others, who were no more helpful in coming up with a reasonable response. I stepped forward with a confidence I didn't possess. "You know what I think? I think you should leave Gallagher alone."

"Why are you protecting him?" Aaron asked at the same time recognition lit in Todd's eyes.

"You two used to be friends." I winced inwardly at Todd's assessment. He narrowed his eyes at me and I braced myself for the inevitable conclusion. If they believed Andy was queer, it wouldn't take much of a leap to think I was too. "But you're not anymore."

John crossed his arms. "So, why protect him now?"

"Consider it for old time's sake. He backed me when I needed it. I'm just returning the favor."

"And what'll you do if we go after him anyway?" John asked.

I speared him with a glare. "You really want to find out?" I couldn't believe it as the lot of them shuffled their feet and averted their gazes. Feeling braver than I had a right, I decided to push my luck. "So, it's settled. No one touches Andy. Ever." I'd waited for nods of acceptance and prayed this wouldn't come back to bite me in the ass. Even if it did, I wouldn't take it back. Andy would always be my best friend, even if I didn't deserve him.

Back in the present, curled up tightly with the man in question, I inhaled the scent of him and hoped that having Andy close would help keep the sins of the past and the nightmares they brought at bay for at least one night.

Andy

I shifted in my sleep and met the resistance of an arm draped across my waist. The hand attached to it coasted along my side to reposition itself higher up. I let out a contented sigh and snuggled back into the steady warmth behind me. My fingers interlaced with the hand's and pulled it closer to my chest. I was hard pressed to come up with a time I'd been more comfortable, more at peace.

The only way this could get any better is if it was actually Mitch curled around me.

My sleepy mind was more than okay with this and happily indulged in the wonderful fantasy that he would hold me so close. The responsible part of my brain that recognized it as morning and that I needed to wake up, had its own reality check: It *was* Mitch and he *wasn't* supposed to be here.

My eyes flew open, and I tossed aside the arm like it had burned me. "Mitch," I hissed in the early morning light streaming mercilessly through the window. It had to be at least seven by now, which meant the first bell for breakfast had already rung.

The rejected arm made a stubborn return and tightened around me like a constrictor. "Go back to sleep, Andy," Mitch mumbled sleepily, nuzzling into my back.

The part of me that desperately wanted to believe the fantasy skipped with joy. The rest of logic, however, would not be denied. "You weren't supposed to fall asleep," I admonished, scooting to the edge and slipping out from under his arm and under the covers. Mitch blinked back at me, not looking nearly as sleepy as he should, though his bed head was rather impressive. I brought my hand up to my own hair, which no doubt looked like I'd had epic sex the night before, which I had, but that was beside the point.

"I think it was warranted." His casual response only got my ruff up further.

"You're not supposed to be here," I argued. "How the hell do you expect to get out of here without drawing any attention?"

"I won't."

I straightened up, my irritation momentarily forgotten in surprise. He slung his legs over the side of the bed and my rebellious eyes couldn't help but drink in every inch of him. He looked damn good in the dark. He looked positively edible in the daylight. I tore my lingering gaze away from his chest and met his unabashed face. "What?"

"Please, Andy, give me a little credit." He walked over to the closet, but not mine, Lucien's. In a matter of seconds, he had an entire uniform laid out, but it wasn't until he slipped on the jacket that I realized the two were nearly the same height. He rolled the sleeves up and tugged the pants as low as they would sit on his hips without falling off. "Not perfect, but it'll do. And since he won't be back until next week, I have plenty of time to return it." He straightened from tying his stolen shoes and looked over at me. "You planning to get dressed?"

My mouth opened and closed again without any words coming out. Mitch's gaze slipped from my face and traveled south. I quickly spun away and started yanking out my own clothes before he could see the reaction his looking at me had. My cheeks burned as long forgotten memories of getting dressed in front of Mitch like it was no big deal resurfaced. We could pretend all we liked, but this was different. We were different.

Deep breath. You can do this. Just stop over-thinking every-thing. Easier said than done, of course.

I finished doing the last button and pulled on my vest, then spun to face Mitch. "There, how do I look?"

He gave a low chuckle and stepped forward, abandoning his perch on Lucien's desk. His fingers slid beneath my folded collar and he used it to pull my mouth to his. We came together with a suction of air that threatened to dissolve my resolve to remain calm and impassive. He deepened the kiss, his tongue slipping past my parted lips to claim what it wanted with abandon, and I could feel myself sliding deeper into the fantasy.

Sex with Mitch was one thing, but this was something else. I wanted to grab him and crush his mouth to mine, to tangle my hands in his hair and hold him as close as possible, to never let him go. I stubbornly kept my rebellious extremities by my side rather than wrap my fingers around his forearms in a caress that would only encourage him. My denied heart twisted painfully in my chest while I continued to kiss him back, unable to stop myself.

I can't do this. I can't be Mitch's friend with benefits. It's killing me. I'm falling in love with him all over again.

I was actually beginning to wonder if I'd ever fallen out of love with him in the first place.

This is just another game for him. What will happen to me when he tires of playing—again?

"Mitch," I said with all the force I could muster.

I have to tell him. I have to stop this.

He pulled back slightly without acknowledging my tone. "You're gonna want to wear your collar up today," he said with a wicked gleam in his eye as he flipped it up.

"What? Why?" I asked, caught off guard by the unusual suggestion.

He leaned forward to whisper in my ear, his lips trailing along my cheek, and my heart skipped. "Because you have a hickey." When he pulled back, his trademark look of mischief danced across his features like Puck himself was looking back at me.

"What?" I raced over to the window to check my reflection and pulled back the now popped collar. Sure enough, a mouth-sized bruise marred the side of my neck. "What the literal hell, Mitch!" Even the collar up barely hid the mark. "Motherfucker."

He laughed while I frantically inspected the hazy image. His response only solidified my earlier assessment that this was all just a game to him.

Does he even understand the ramifications of what he did? What it means?

He'd marked me, like a possession. I was literally branded…as his. My stomach fluttered. I ruthlessly murdered all the butterflies and refused to acknowledge that being marked by Mitch was in any way something I wanted.

"Are you trying to get me in trouble?" I asked, still inspecting the mark.

"Keep," he corrected.

I spun around to face him, stunned for the fourth time that morning and yet again at a loss for words.

"Keep you in trouble," he added with a devious smile.

"I'm gonna murder you." After all, I'd already massacred a rabble of butterflies. What was my best friend?

"Yeah?" Mischief sparkled in his eyes that showed zero signs of remorse for what he'd done as he inched his way toward the door.

I mirrored his movement. "Yeah."

His laughter rang out as he spun and raced for the door. It flew open, and he tore out of the room. I sprinted after him, grabbing my scarf on the way out and resigned to return for my satchel after I murdered him. We sped down the corridor toward the dining hall. With his long legs, he should have had more of a lead, but I gained ground even as I wrapped the scarf around my neck to hide the evidence of our night together. A giddy joy I hadn't experienced in years filled my chest and fueled my limbs.

Abruptly, Mitch skidded to a halt. Confused, I looked ahead to see what could have caused such a reaction and barely saw the teacher in time to do the same. Professor Stein quirked an eyebrow at us as we walked sedately past him side by side. I did what I could to school my ridiculous grin, but could do nothing about the excitement running rampant inside me.

"Gentleman," he said flatly.

"Professor Stein," we echoed in unison.

The hallway was abnormally quiet as we continued to walk. Mitch glanced over his shoulder several times before finally catching my eye. My grin finally broke free, and we sprinted in tandem all the way to breakfast.

Chapter 24

Mitch

I leaned against the wall with my arms crossed and hoped I didn't look too conspicuous. A few students wandered the halls, some I recognized from my classes, others I didn't. While Ulwich was a legacy school, not everyone could stay. Some moved, some got transferred. Whatever the reason they left, they rarely came back. Part of me envied them, another part recognized that if my Uncle Teri hadn't gotten me in at Ulwich, I never would have met Andy.

A door further down the hall opened as another class let out for the day. Luckily, it was a group of lower classmen and none of my teammates. The memory of the last time I'd run into them like this made me wince and I shifted my gaze back to the door of Garza's classroom.

Finally, it opened. Andy filled the doorway, and I stood straighter, a smile already tugging at my lips, though he hadn't seen me yet. He was glancing over his shoulder, still talking to Garza. I bit my lip to stop myself from shouting at him to hurry already and prevent the grin in danger of cracking my face. While he continued talking, I let my gaze travel down his body, appreciating the way his buttoned blazer accentuated his slim shoulders and highlighted his waist. Not everyone could pull off the academy uniform, but Andy wore it well.

The navy blazer made his copper hair that much brighter and paired well with his ivory freckled skin. Of course, I'd rather be peeling him *out* of the uniform, but that was beside the point. It didn't hurt that Andy *always* looked good either. Even the way the unremarkable khakis hugged his trim waist and ended in a perfect cuff just before his polished Oxford loafers set my pulse racing. Or maybe that had more to do with his legs. They may not be as long as mine, but they'd been able to wrap around me just fine. And *that* was a feeling I wouldn't soon forget.

"Sure thing, professor, I'll get right on that," Andy said as he stepped through the door. The heavy wood swung shut, and Andy lifted his gaze. When it landed on me, a smile instantly blossomed on his face and glowed in his eyes. "Hey, what are you doing here?"

I fought the urge to close the distance separating us and snare him with a kiss. Instead, I shrugged. "Thought it was a nice enough afternoon and wondered if you'd be interested in going for a walk. We could head toward town or stick to the woods. Whatever." I had to bite my tongue to stop babbling. That wasn't a problem I normally had, but considering how well everything had been going since we'd slept together, I was worried about messing things up. I still couldn't get over how easy it had been between us. I'd expected full on awkward or for Andy to withdraw, but he hadn't. He'd continued to tutor me in physics and even helped with my recent Lit paper. It was likely we'd turned a corner, and as much as I wanted more from Andy, I also didn't want to do anything to jeopardize the progress we *had* made.

"It is a nice day, isn't it? I suppose I could go for a walk." He gave me a quick once over, no doubt taking in the fact that I was already in jeans, a knitted sweater, and a jacket. "I'll change real quick. Meet you at the wall?"

"Sure thing."

A whopping ten minutes later, Andy walked up to our usual spot, and I had to remind myself to breathe. He looked positively edible in a forest green cable-knit sweater that was definitely heavier than mine and skin-tight jeans so dark blue they might as well be black. If I'd wanted to greet him with a kiss before, I wanted to drag him into the woods and devour him now.

"That was fast," I said, grateful my voice didn't pitch like my stomach did as he stepped close enough to smell his herbal scent.

He gave me a cheeky grin. "Well, my mentor meeting with Garza went longer than expected and the sun sets earlier now. Hope you weren't waiting too long."

"Nope," I lied as we fell in step and angled for the edge of the woods. I glanced at him again and worked diligently to keep my dirty thoughts of rucking up his sweater and leaving hickeys all over his torso to myself. "You gonna be warm enough?"

"I was literally sweating as I left the school. Far as I'm concerned, this feels great."

I shook my head. The winter chill had set in with a vengeance, and we'd already had snow twice. But I also didn't want to point out that I remembered how easily he got cold...or the fact that he'd just shivered. "I kind of feel like an ass for not asking sooner, but how's the mentorship going?"

Andy darted me a quick look, surprise dominating his small smile. "It's going really well. My grades are all up—"

I rolled my eyes. "No surprise there."

"Shut up," he said with a chuckle that only fed the light filling me. "Like I was saying, grades are good. I'm on my way to being valedictorian, though it seems I have a little competition there."

I frowned, my eyebrows pinching together. The idea of *anyone* out-smarting Andy was ludicrous. "Really? Who?"

"Price, if you can believe it."

"No fucking way."

Andy nodded, though he didn't look like he believed it himself. "Way. But I'm not really worried. It's not like I *need* to be valedictorian." He shot me a glare as I guffawed. "What's so funny?"

"Can I get that in writing? Tell me with a straight face that you won't do everything short of cheating to make sure that title goes to you." I lifted my eyebrows as I waited.

He rolled his shoulders, and his beautiful mouth twisted into a scowl. "Fine. I will. But only because it will look great on my final transcript."

"Oh yeah, *that's* the reason," I teased. He bumped me with his shoulder and I was tempted to wrap an arm around him to keep him close. It would also help to stave off the shivering he would adamantly refuse to admit he was doing. Except with the school not that far off and students wandering around in search of early evening plans, here wasn't as safe or free as I would like. "So, um, you know which university you're going to?"

"Yes!" Andy quickly glanced around as several startled birds took flight. "I mean, yes," he repeated in a softer tone, that did nothing to diminish his enthusiasm. "I've already submitted to Chicago University. Garza is making me apply to some backups, so I'll be doing that over winter break. But, honestly, it's Chicago or bust for me. Now all I'm waiting on is for Garza to finalize his letter of recommendation and hopefully my acceptance letter, though he says they like to drag their feet to make applicants sweat."

"I have every belief you'll get in. How could they not want you?"

Andy gave me a sheepish smile, and my heart did a silly flip. "You really think so?"

"Do you really have to ask?" I responded softly.

He let out a self-deprecating laugh. "No, I suppose not." He glanced at me again, this time a light of curiosity in his eyes. "I know it's a sensitive topic, but what about you? I know that Santinelli is almost everyone on the team's mentor, but do *you* have any colleges you'd like to go to?"

My steps slowed as I turned his words over in my head. I really hadn't given it much thought and even with my grades being better, my chances of getting accepted somewhere weren't great. Plus, without a scholarship, no way could my mom afford it, and there wasn't a chance I was letting my uncle foot the bill for that too, not after covering Ulwich's steep tuition. I came to a full stop and considered Andy, an idea forming. Chicago had a lacrosse team. They weren't a big name in the sport by any means and I doubted coach would have encouraged any of their scouts to visit, but that didn't mean one couldn't.

Andy stood watching me, having stopped when I did. He wrapped his arms tightly around his torso and gave a full body shudder.

"That's it, enough of this."

"Enough of what?" he asked, his teeth chattering on the "t".

I slipped off my jacket and held it out for him. "You're obviously cold, Andy, and I'm not gonna stand by while you stubbornly pretend you're not. Now turn around."

"But—"

"No buts." I shook the jacket for emphasis. He pouted and grumbled under his breath something about me being obstinate, but turned and let me help him into the still warm sleeves. I hiked it over his shoulders and he spun back to face me, still scowling. "There. Now, isn't that better?" The jacket fit me perfectly, but it nearly swallowed Andy whole. I chuckled to myself at how freaking adorable he looked in the oversized outerwear and pulled the lapels tighter.

Andy gazed up at me, his green eyes bright beneath his copper lashes, his cheeks pink from the cold, and his lips parted as if he'd planned to say something.

My heart hammered as I smoothed the front of the jacket over his chest and stared back at him. Forget dragging him into the woods to make out. I wanted to kiss him here, right now, witnesses be damned. How had I gone so long without his lips on mine? When I'd given into the impulse four years ago, it had been more than enough to make me want them all the time. But I'd been scared. And I'd wasted so much time.

"Mitch?"

Hearing Andy whisper my name helped me reach the conclusion I should have reached all those years ago. He deserved the truth. "Andy, I... I need to tell you something—I should have told you a long time ago—about us. Me, really." I hesitated, my gaze fixed on where my thumb rubbed along the zipper, still anxious despite knowing this was the right thing. "I owe you the truth. I—"

"It's okay, Mitch. I know."

I flicked my gaze up to meet his, my breath catching even as my heart threatened to explode out of my chest. "You do?"

"Yeah." He gave me a soft smile and took a small step back, causing my hands to fall free of him. "I get it. You're curious. This isn't really you, and I'm… I'm okay with that. Really."

I was pretty sure my brain was leaking out of my ears, because I had no idea what he was talking about. With a shake of my head, I stepped closer. "Please, let me finish. You deserve an apology."

Andy

How naïve could I be? Sleeping together didn't magically erase who Mitch was… Who I was. This was always doomed. We would never work. Mitch would never be *mine*. And yet, I'd childishly let myself indulge in the fantasy and hoped we had more time before we had to confront this conversation.

I took a deep breath and tried not to let my hurt show as I put on a front of acceptance. "Seriously, Mitch, there's nothing to apologize for. Like I've said before, I knew what I was doing. There's no need to let me down easy." Despite my valiant effort to maintain eye contact, I couldn't do it *and* suppress the stinging building behind my eyes. I dropped my gaze to look past his shoulder, where I wouldn't have to see his confused expression. I didn't have it in me to break this down for him. He was experimenting, I got it. There was no need to make this more painful than it already was. He was straight. I was not. Nothing was ever going to change that.

"Andy, please, just listen to me. I should have been upfront with you years ago, but I'm not brave like you are. You trusted me with your truth, and I should have trusted you with mine. I'm—"

I wasn't really listening; it was too painful. Why couldn't we have continued pretending? Why did it have to come to this?

Movement behind him caught my attention. I squinted and instinctively leaned forward to make it out. The indistinct shadows solidified into the outline of several people. "Oh shit," I hissed, then promptly dove into the trees. No way was I letting Mitch get caught by his homophobic teammates on what probably looked like an intimate walk with me.

"What the fuck?" he asked, stepping closer to the shrub I'd ducked behind. "What are you doing?" He leaned down like he was going to come after me despite my waving for him to go. Then a braying laugh, like a hyena with the flu, cut through the otherwise peaceful landscape, and Mitch straightened to look back the way we'd come. The noise came again and Mitch cursed under his breath. For as long as I lived, I doubt I'd ever be able to forget John's God awful laugh.

"Yo, Hudson! What are you doing out here all on your lonesome?" a voice I was pretty sure belonged to Kyle asked. Given that the only thing I could see from my vantage was Mitch's back, all I had was guesswork.

Mitch's gaze flicked to my hiding spot, and I held my breath. Then he moved closer to the voices. Fortunately, his response masked my sigh of relief. "Figured I'd take my happy ass for a walk, take in the fresh air. It was nice until you bozos showed up." He laughed, but there was no joy in it.

"Well, you look like a loser, wandering around by yourself." Judging by the wheezy laugh that followed, that had to be John.

"A cold loser," maybe Aaron added.

Mitch shrugged. "Don't know what you mean. Feels great out here to me." My hands reflexively curled around the opening of

Mitch's jacket around me. He'd been dead-on about me being cold, but I should have been more adamant about refusing. Except it had felt good to have someone take care of me, to have *Mitch* take care of me.

"We're headed to town to hang at the arcade. Join us." *That* was definitely Brian Daniels, and it wasn't a request. Even from my limited perspective, I could see Mitch's shoulders stiffen.

Several beats filled the silence until I wanted to burst from the woods like some kind of jack-in-the-box, just to cut the tension. At last Mitch said cooler than I would have been able to, "Sure. Sounds like a good time." Then he stepped aside and held up an arm. "Lead the way."

The sound of footsteps grew louder until I caught glimpses of the group. Per my suspicions, Brian, Kyle, John, Aaron, and to my surprise, Nathaniel, Mitch's roommate, were all there. Mitch let most of them past and only turned to fall in line when he was even with Nathaniel. He glanced in my direction again, a strange mix of emotion on his face, and shrugged one shoulder, offering me a half smile that didn't touch his eyes, as if to say, "What can I do?"

I remained perfectly still as I waited for them all to leave. Once they were too far to make out clearly, I stood and started making my way back to the school, careful to stay in the trees and out of sight. I clutched Mitch's jacket tighter around me, both to stave off the cold and to inhale what lingered of his warmth. Even as his tangy scent soothed my nerves, my heart cracked.

How could I have been so foolish as to let Mitch back in? Being friends again was one thing, but fooling around was not only dangerous to my heart but our physical wellbeing. Tears that I told myself I would never cry again spilled free to chill on my cheeks. Would I even be able to push Mitch back to arm's length now that he was back in my life? Whether or not I could was beside the point—I had to. And I had all winter break to figure out how.

Acknowledgments

For as much joy as it has brought me, writing the first installment of Mitch and Andy's story has not been easy. Luckily, I've had an amazing support team and group of beta readers that has helped this story excel. Thanks to the valuable insights from Mx Alex and Gavin, I can go forward confident that my characters are being represented as complete individuals, beautiful in their complexity. Special thanks to Chloe Kincaid, who has adored these two as much as I have and been the most amazing cheerleader. To M.L. Eaden, thank you for not letting me give up when publishing this book felt like only an empty dream. And to Goose, for stepping out of your comfort zone to provide a unique perspective, I'll always be grateful.

I couldn't have done it without any of you!

A Sneak Peek at

Calvin & Benny's story

Our Secret Winter

The empty pudding cup sat beside me on the grass, forgotten as I leaned forward to give the match below my full attention. With the arrival of the school's key Midfielder and two Defenders, the friendly game had evolved into a full-on practice match. No pads or helmets meant the body checks stayed fairly tame, but you wouldn't find me complaining. The sweaty bodies below glistened in the afternoon sun, a veritable feast for my eyes. It never ceased to amaze me how a school consumed with homophobia didn't see how shoving a bunch of developing boys in close proximity to each other wouldn't foster at least a little exploration.

Andy, my companion and only real friend in this hellhole of repression, had long since abandoned me. Lacrosse held no interest for him. Surprising, considering the star player had once been his best friend and seemed determined to be so again. I winced as a Middie and an Attackman came together hard enough to be heard even from this distance. Benjamin Price stared down at his latest victim, who remained on the ground in what was likely a state of shock. With his broad shoulders, thick torso, and muscular legs, Benny was a beast on and off the field. A veritable Laocoön or Farnese Heracles. My fingers tingled as I ran through the list of Grecian sculptures and imagined running them over the living model currently dominating the game.

What I wouldn't give to get my hands on that.

…Again.

A smile curved my mouth as I scooped the fallen art supplies back into my bag along with the cleaned pudding cup and spoon. I straightened up and cast a glance back down at the field below. The poor Attackman had found his feet, and the match had resumed, though it was clearly winding down. They'd be heading to the showers at the locker room next. If I meandered my way along, I'd arrive just in time for my appointment, and if I was lucky, a peek at all that exquisite flesh.

I yanked my loose tie off and stuffed it in my bag, where it hung out like a mustard striped navy tongue. Next, I undid several buttons and yanked on the stifling collar. The uniform they made us to endure was just another symbol of the oppression forced upon us and one I openly rebelled against. I rolled the cuffs of the navy jacket, exposing the white satin underlining, and pushed back the hair that had fallen in my face. The tight curls hung substantially longer than code dictated and were a constant nuisance. But it was either tie them back or cut them off, both of which were tantamount to admitting defeat. Unsurprisingly, the damn things tumbled back in my face and stuck to the sweat dampening my forehead. Not that I was out of shape, far from it, but the way was long and the afternoon exceedingly warm.

At last, my destination came into view. Rather than venture into the locker room proper to enjoy the view and AC, I sought out a bit of shade off to the side and waited for my quarry to emerge. The coolness of the painted cement offered a welcome reprieve from the heat and a convenient lean-to. I fished out a sketchbook and pencil, and made sure the rest of what I would need was within easy reach.

The pale cream of the fresh rag paper held all the promise of creation and none of the inspiration. I blew out a breath and stared at the soft white canvas. If I couldn't round out my portfolio, then I might as well kiss my chance at the Art Institute of Chicago good-bye. Of course, there was always Yale, but Chicago held my heart. I glared resentfully at the stubbornly blank page and graphite poised above it.

You'd think drawing people would be easy for me, considering how many I see all the time.

But not the way Jankowski wants them, layered with nuances of vulnerability and authenticity.

Therein lie the rub, while I could see those things in others, translating it to canvas meant exposing a part of myself I'd locked away since I was nine.

And some doors should never be opened.

With a disparaging grunt, I fell back on tried and true. By the time my appointment arrived, my rendition of a Quaking Aspen was in full form on the once pristine page. I glanced up out of the corner of my eye without raising my head. My perch in the shade lay far enough from the main entrance to be inconspicuous and mostly hidden from view—unless, of course, you were looking for me.

Brian went rigid as he spied me lurking in the shadows. After a beat, he made his way over, movements jerky like an automaton in sore need of oil. His stunningly dark skin, an intriguing mix of Vandyke Brown with Medium Hansa Yellow undertones, at once absorbed and reflected the afternoon sun. As one of the only other students of color in our grade, it was a true shame he hadn't been able to look past my orientation to foster any kind of friendship or camaraderie.

"Bridges," he grumbled under his breath as he stopped close enough to be heard, but far enough to deny association. I smirked as I took my time putting away my sketchpad with exaggerated care. The longer I took, the more growly he became. It was no secret Brian didn't like me, of course, he'd liked me even less since I'd caught him and another boy giving each other hand jobs.

At last, I procured the pack of smokes from my bag. His eyes lit up, then immediately darted around to make sure no prying ones were nearby. He reached out and I pulled the open carton back out of reach. "Payment first."

His face twisted and his hand fell back to his side. "I don't have it."

Cute how they always think I don't know.

"Don't be coy, darling." He winced at the endearment, and my lips tweaked up in a wicked half smile. "Post came yesterday and someone got a delivery." I held out a hand and waited patiently. He ground his teeth and grumbled incoherent insults as he liberated a small wrapped package from his bag. He plopped it rudely in my hand and glared daggers at me.

"Happy, you damn fairy?"

"Immensely." I curled my fingers around the vacuum sealed box and held out the carton of cigarettes with a few greener companions nestled inside. He snatched them from me and didn't bother to check the contents before shoving the poor, abused packaging into his bag. "Pleasure doing business with you."

"Fuck off," he sneered.

"Is that an invitation?" I batted my lashes as I pocketed the high-end cosmetics. It wasn't my fault he had connections to the esteemed company through his sister. Now, whether he stole, bought, or somehow coerced her into gifting the expensive items, I had no idea, nor did I care. It clearly was worth the price, since this was by no means our first such deal.

He rolled his eyes without deigning to answer, then turned to stomp sullenly off with his contraband.

"Oh, do tell Tanner I said hello," I called out before he could get too far.

Brian stiffened once more, confirming my suspicion that the two hadn't ceased their extracurriculars despite being caught. Of course, I'd never out either of them on principle, but Brian didn't know that nor would he likely believe me if I told him as much. Plus, it was nice to remind him he was not as untouchable as he acted. He stole a few moments to pull himself together, then resumed storming off.

I chuckled to myself, pleased with a good day's work and content with the knowledge that my client base was well and truly in line. Secrets were a dime a dozen in this place if you paid attention, and most definitely did. A deeper shadow fell across me, briefly dimming my merriment. Curious if it was another client in need of a trade or a new petitioner, I glanced up once more.

Ah, the latter.

"Benjamin." Nothing could be done to school the wicked grin that stretched my cheeks. Sadly, I didn't seem to have anything he couldn't acquire on his own, not to mention the only secret I had on him fell squarely in the sacred column. I straightened up from my slouched repose to be of an even height with him, but didn't abandon my casual stance. "Fancy seeing you here. What can I do for you? Any particular needs I could help you with?"

The slight tightening around his eyes was the only indication he'd caught the targeted emphasis. "What are you doing here? You know your queer ass isn't allowed anywhere near the locker rooms."

I pushed off the wall to invade the fringe of his personal bubble, undeterred by the hostility and a touch emboldened by the fact that he'd sought me out. "There's no such rule against it."

"There is if I say there is, you fucking fagot."

"Ooh…" I shook my head from side to side. "Tsk tsk. You sure you wanna do this, Benny? Here," I purred. "All alone, without your boys to back you up? Last time I checked, you liked to have…a hand." Shuttered fear danced behind his eyes as he no doubt remembered something he tried hard to forget. Meanwhile, the same memory was emblazoned in gold and given a position of prominence in a hall of fucking glory in my mind. "That's what I thought. Now, if you'll excuse me, I have other business to attend to."

Unable to resist riling him up more, I lazily dragged my gaze down his body. Once more, the fantasy of molding that incredible physique in smooth, wet, pliable clay filled my thoughts and made my fingers itch to reach out and test the firm muscle before me, if only to make sure I got the consistency right. By the time my gaze found his face once more, his ears burned a fantastic Alizarin Red with steam practically billowing out of them while he fought not to swallow his tongue.

I winked and blew him a kiss, which he didn't catch. "See you around, Benny." I walked past him close enough to feel the tension and anger radiating off his statue-like form. No more slurs followed me as I made my way back to the school proper to inform my next client I had their supply.

About the Author

Sam Bolanos (she/they) is a genderqueer author and founder of Chaotic Neutral Press LLC. They believe in love, equality, and the Oxford comma. When not playing with her three dogs, who you can follow on Instagram @austendogs, or spending time with her incredible husband, she's probably agonizing over edits or escaping into her latest fantasy.

Welcome to the adventure!

Newsletter: subscribe
Website: Booksbysbolanos.com
Facebook: @Booksbysbolanos
Twitter: @Booksbysbolanos
Instagram: @sbolanosbooks

Series

Paranormal Stories

War on Darkness
Darkness Defined (MM)
Order of Light (MM)
Knights of Nyx (MM)

Moons of Mystery
Sara's Moon (MF)
Charline's Solstice (MF)
Diana's Eclipse (MF)

<u>Contemporary Romances</u>

Ulwich Preparatory Academy
Our Last Fall (MM)
Our Secret Winter (MM)
Our Epic Spring (MM)

Oak Haven Romance
One Brave Thing (Enby/M)
All the Hype (MM)